MW00423836

THE ORIGINAL LOST BOY

Heroes aren't always what they seem.

By: C.L. Bush

Printed in the United States of America

First Printing, 2017

ISBN 9781521173343

www.clbush.com/

OTHER BOOKS BY C.L. BUSH

Fire In My Heart Series:

The Heart of Now – Book One

Fire of My Past – Book Two

Wife of Tomorrow – Book Three

A Hand in Love and Murder – Book Four

A Trial of Secrets – Book Five

A Vindicated Heart – Book Six

Major Series:

Major Bodyguard – Book One

Major Pacifier – Book Two

Major Charming – Book Three

Stand Alones:

Alice and Uncas

Echo of Whispers Series:

Echo of Whispers – Book One

*I F*cking Love Coloring Series:*

Mandala 1st Edition

Mandala 2nd Edition

American/UK Cuss Word Edition

A big thank you to my contributor Megan Stradley! Your help was immensely appreciated □

And also to my amazing editor, Sarah Burgess. You take my brain and make it readable. Thank you!

TABLE OF CONTENTS

CHAPTER ONE

CHAPTER TWO

CHAPTER THREE

CHAPTER FOUR

CHAPTER FIVE

CHAPTER SIX

CHAPTER SEVEN

CHAPTER EIGHT

CHAPTER NINE

CHAPTER TEN

CHAPTER ELEVEN

CHAPTER TWELVE

CHAPTER THIRTEEN

EPILOGUE

ABOUT THE AUTHOR

What if you found out that one of your favorite heroes from childhood was no hero at all, but a villain? Peter Pan had a way of spinning tales and manipulating the truth in his favor, and that's what this story is about. It's about the true Peter Pan. If you want to remain blissfully ignorant and continue to believe Peter Pan was a great guy who rescued lost boys and gave them a home, then I would advise you to put this book down.

If you want to know the truth, however, then I implore you to turn this first page and read the story of how I met Peter Pan. Be warned that everything you thought you once knew is about to be changed forever.

CHAPTER ONE

Pan first visited me in my dreams, in the dead of night after I had been rocked to sleep by the Atlantic waves lazily brushing against the boat and causing it to sway from side to side. His bright, forest green eyes gazed deeply into mine and I watched his lips move in a familiar rhythm of words without being able to hear or understand them. The corners of his mouth were always curved up slightly. The pocket watch resting in his breast pocket chimed and I watched him take it out to check the time. The back of the watch was smooth gold, but the cover was mostly carved away save for the mystical gear-like designs. The outer ring was pure gold with impressions of stars and moons circling around and around and around. I always found myself entranced by the cover.

As the last chime faded away, I awoke. The rocking of my father's ship had lulled me into a peaceful slumber the night before, but now the sound of the gulls crying by the port window forced me to open my eyes to the harsh sunlight of a day already started. Father would expect me up and ready to go just like the rest of the crew. We were sailing back from the west indies, a boon of trade in what is now known as the Victorian era.

I had been with him on his ship *The Land Gazer* for the past six months, my parents having agreed I was old enough to learn the ways of the family business. I was not thrilled. What they didn't tell me is that I wouldn't be going back home. My mother was ill. Her skin growing pale and sallow, her hair lying limp, as the days sucked the life from her while she struggled to breath.

Years later now I regret that I pushed her hug away so quickly as an eleven-year-old boy excited to break from his mother's apron strings and have his first adventure.

I never put much thought into the mysterious stranger who visited in my sleep. Most mornings, I could barely remember the encounter and shrugged it off as some weird dream. That was why I never thought twice about why after a full night's sleep, I would wake the next day feeling like a zombie.

My father sure noticed, though. My father was a seaman, a captain of his own trading ship. He knew boats in and out and was desperate to pass that knowledge on to his only son, to me. So, whenever I acted sluggishly or seemingly not paying attention, this would infuriate the man.

"James!" he would shout. I learned whenever he shouted to click my heels together, stand straight, and press the palms of my hands into my thighs, gazing up at him with the utmost respect. "I told you to drop anchor!" I would provide Father with one stern nod and move on to the task ordered.

After we had docked the boat at the Thames in London, England, we headed into town. It was all part of Father's *father and son bonding summer sailing trip*. The purpose of the trip was to teach me about sailing, which I never thought would come in handy, to show me the world, and of course, to bond. Since Father was a captain, he had been absent most of my life. The trip was his way of trying to make up for the lost time.

I didn't appreciate it back then, but I wish I had. I wish I'd put in the same amount of effort into getting to know him as he put into teaching me the ins and outs of a boat. If only I had known then what was in store for me, I wouldn't have taken a second with my father for granted. I would have kissed my mother's cheek and hugged her tightly before our trip instead of giving her the cold shoulder for making me go on the trip with my father like a spoiled brat. I would have been a better son.

We sat at a rotted wooden table in the pub. My father's mug frothed over with his ale. After taking a few deep swigs of his drink, foam dripped from his thick black mustache. "What is goin' on with ya, boy?" he asked.

His eyes drilled into mine in a way only a sergeant's could. His eyes were black as coal. It was impossible to tell where his pupil ended and his irises began. He got this crinkle on his forehead whenever he tried to figure out how something worked. And he was always, always so serious!

I looked him straight in the eyes, even though the weight of his gaze always made me squirm just slightly. "I'm not sure what you're talking about, sir."

He narrowed his eyes. "C'mon, I've noticed how your head's always in the clouds. I ask you to do something and your mind is lost in Wonderland!"

I resisted the urge to shrug, which was practically a sin to Father. "I'm sorry. I will try harder."

His face softened just slightly then. He broke eye contact with a sigh. He lifted his mug, gauging how much was left with his right eye, before bringing the rim to his lips and sucking the ale dry. He gasped for air as he slammed the empty mug onto the table. "I'm trying, James."

Seeing my father behave so brazenly was such an unusual sight that all I could do was watch.

"I'm trying to understand you. Really, I am." He paused to let his long black hair loose and run his fingers through his mane. "I know I haven't been around much." His black eyes met mine once again. "But I can tell something isn't right."

There was a long, uncomfortable silence between us, only lessened by the hooting and hollering of other drunken lads at the bar. It took a couple of beats before I realized it was my turn to talk again. "I've been really tired lately?"

"Are you having trouble sleeping?" he quickly asked, the ale taking no effect on the sharpness of his mind.

"No. I mean, maybe?"

"Well, which is it?"

"I don't know. I'm just tired."

The conversation was making me more anxious and tired than I had been in the past few days since the dreams had started. Of course, I hadn't put two and two together yet. Don't worry, I'll get to what the two and two are soon.

He gave me one last leery glance before slamming his hand down between us, making me jump from my seat. "Barkeep!" His voice boomed over all other noise in the pub and someone quickly appeared to take our dirty dishes.

Father dished out some coins and then we walked the dark London streets back to our boat. She wasn't anything amazing or extravagant. A simple wooden boat with three masses that had enough room for Father, me, and the small crew of five men. That was all we needed for the trip we were taking. We boarded together.

I was prepared to head to my sleeping corridors when father put his heavy, warm hand on my shoulder. "Tonight, son, you learn to navigate with the stars."

He pulled me to the nose of the boat where he usually steered the wheel himself. From his deep pockets, he pulled out something cylinder. In one fluent motion, he shook the device, and it grew three times its size. He brought the small end to his eye and he peered through the telescope. After gazing at the sky for a few moments, he passed the handheld device to me.

"What do you see?" he asked.

Mimicking him, I brought the small end to my right eye and peered through the glass. After searching for patterns for a while, my eyes finally connected the dots. "I see a horse."

I looked up at Father to see him nodding in approval. "That would be the constellation Major. If you can see that constellation, do you know what direction we're looking in?"

Instinctively I shook my head, then I quickly added, "No, sir."

"That means we're facing northwest. If our next destination is France, what direction do we need to be heading?"

"Southeast?"

He nodded again, his lips curved up with a hint of a smile. "That's correct. Do you know what constellation we would see if we were looking southeast?"

"No, sir."

"I'll give you an easy one. Look for the constellation Aquarius. It'll look like a lasso."

Again, I put the telescope to my eye and searched for a cluster of stars that remotely looked like a lasso. Slowly, I moved around in a circle. My eyes followed a line of stars until they separated into a jagged circle.

Excitedly, I shouted, "Father, I found it! It's in that direction!" I pulled the telescope from my face to look up at Father, but he was no longer next to me.

"Good job, lad!" he called to me from the other end of the boat where he was preparing the

sails. "Why don't you come back here and give me a hand so we can set sail?"

"Yes, sir."

Before I knelt down to help him with the ropes, I offered him back his telescope. He closed my fingers back around the cool metal. "No, son. You hold onto it. I will need your help to keep us on the right path."

I nodded my head once again before slipping it into the deep pockets of my slacks. Together, we prepared the boat for our next voyage and set sail for Italy.

Once we were on a smooth path, Father released me from my duties. "I think I can take it from here, son. Why don't you try to get some real sleep?"

For once, I didn't mind helping Father and his men sail the boat. Seeking out different constellations to navigate by was like playing a game. I didn't want to go to sleep. I wanted to know more about what else was out there. The disappointment must have been written on my face because Father sighed heavily, his eyes still on the calm waters before us.

"There is a book in my nightstand. It goes over all the constellations, where they can be seen on different parts of the earth, during different parts of the year. Why don't you read it over? Study it, so you can help me out again another night."

"Yes, sir." I eagerly ran to our sleeping corridors and pulled open the drawer in his nightstand. Inside, sitting atop some other papers and journals, was a black, leather-bound book. The title was pressed into the cover in gold letters, *The Constellations*. It was thick, but small enough that it fit inside my jacket pocket. Whenever I wasn't reading through it or making notes on the margin of the pages, I always kept it close to me in my breast pocket. I still do.

Not all days with Father went that well. He often flipped flopped between an irate man who thought I was good-for-nothing to the calm man who was patient with me and wanted to take the time to teach me new things and actually get to know me. I quickly learned the differences were night and day, literally. At night, the ale he gulped down like water actually calmed the beast within. It was in the morning, the next day, that the ale came back with a vengeance and he became a roaring monster. I learned to take advantage of our nighttime voyages and to stay out of his way as much as possible while the sun was still out and he hadn't taken his first sip of a frothy beer.

Later, I learned that I couldn't always trust my memories. Pan had a way of infiltrating the mind. To this day, I don't know if what I remember is always what really happened.

Of course, that plan couldn't have worked forever. Eventually, I was going to get on his nerves by saying the wrong thing or moving the wrong way. That time caught up with us quickly as we headed away from Italy and were on our way to Greece.

"James! James!" Father was at the point of screaming my name before I heard him.

I jerked my head up, lifting my eyes from tracing and memorizing the constellations in my black book to find Father's black eyes glaring back at me.

"Didn't you hear me?" His voice boomed through the still morning air.

"No, sir."

"What are you doing over here?" His eyes fell to the book gripped tightly in my hands. He yanked it away from me, scowling.

Without a thought, I yelled out in protest.

His scowl worsened, the wrinkles around his frown deepened and his thick, black brows burrowed together. "I didn't give you this book so you could laze around all day," he hissed.

"I'm sorry, sir."

His nose crinkled. "I asked you to tighten the sail. We need to change direction slightly. The winds are changing."

"Yes, Sir." I ran to the tail. I latched onto the wildly flying rope, but the wind was too strong. It yanked the rope from my hands, despite my tight grip. I hissed as pain shot through my hands.

Father shoved me out of the way, pushing me so hard I fell onto the deck. I landed hands-first to keep from hitting my head and cried out as my burnt hands brushed against the old splintered wood.

"Can't you do anything right?"

I watched as he secured the rope, snapping the sail into place, and securely tied it down. Once he had cleaned up my mess so to speak, he directed his rage at me once again.

He stomped over to where I was still lying on the dock. He grabbed my wrist and yanked me onto my feet so fast I heard it pop. Without a word, he swung his hand back and I watched in slow motion as his open palm flung at me, meeting my cheek with a smack. I brought my aching hands up to my burning cheek. Despite trying my hardest to keep a straight face, my bottom lip trembled.

"What is your purpose if you can't even perform a simple task?" When I didn't reply, he pushed my shoulder. "Huh? Answer me!"

"I... I don't know." I tried to keep my voice even, but I could hear the words slur and stutter off my tongue.

"Neither do I."

A hot tear sizzled from underneath my eyelids and dropped from my lashes. I tried to will it to slide back in, but it continued to fall down my throbbing cheek.

"What, you're going to cry now? Why don't you grow up! Real men don't cry."

He threw my book at my chest. My hands fumbled to catch it, and it fell before my feet.

He snorted. "Pathetic."

I knelt down to retrieve it from the ground. Tears clouded my vision.

With Father's back facing me, he breathed, "Get out of my sight."

I fled to my sleeping corridors and sat on the edge of my bed. I rested the back of my hands on my knees, my red throbbing palms face up. Next to my bed, I had some handkerchiefs Mum had sent on the trip with me. They were white satin with a J sewed into the corner. I took two of the handkerchiefs and wrapped up my hands. No matter how hard I tried to keep the sobs from shaking my ribs, tears still fumbled from underneath my eyelids and fell onto my wrapped palms, the fabric soaking them up. I took a deep breath, tucking my book into my breast pocket, and laid down.

Father's words echoed in the deepest parts of my mind. *Why don't you grow up! Real men don't cry.* His voice continued, over and over again on a loop. These were the words that would continue to haunt me, even to this day.

I felt a lot of emotions that afternoon. I was angry with Mum for pushing me to go on the trip. I was angry she didn't let me stay home, that she thought a boy had to bond with his father or how else would be become a proper man? Most of all, though, I felt alone. I felt lost. Maybe I was good-for-nothing after all. Perhaps, Father was right and all I would ever do was screw up.

I fell asleep as the overwhelming sense of being misplaced washed over me and Father's words continued to play on a loop in the back of my head. Would I ever find my place in the world?

***

My eyelids were still sealed shut as I heard Father shuffling around the corridor. It sounded as if he were pacing back and forth before my bed. As I continued to push away the fog of sleep, I realized the footsteps I heard were far too light to be Father's. My eyelids snapped open, and I gaped at the boy at the end of my bed.

He had dark, messy strawberry blonde hair that stood up in odd places. I appeared as if his undershirt was made of netting and his vest was sewn together with odd, tattered pieces of leather and thick fabric. It looked like he had taken a pair of men's slacks and tried to make them his own His slacks were rolled up at the waist and ankles. His clothes were torn in some places and patched up with other miscellaneous odds and ends.

From the pocket of his slacks, he pulled out his gold pocket watch to check the time. That was when it clicked in my mind that I had seen this boy before.

"Who are you?" I asked in awe.

His vibrant green eyes looked up at me and his thin lips spread into a wide smile. "Oh, good. You're awake!"

I shook my head. Maybe it was still all a dream. I dropped my face in my wrapped hands. The fabric was soft against my skin. I was awake.

"Who are you?" I asked again.

If possible, his grin only grew. He stood with his chest proud and fists on his hips as he announced, "I'm Peter Pan."

CHAPTER TWO

Once I had gotten a name, I only had more questions. "Why are you dressed like that? Where did you come from? How did you get on our boat? Why are you standing in front of my bed?"

He shrugged as if it were all very simple. "I'm standing here because you haven't invited me to sit yet." Then he sat down at the edge of my bed.

"What are you doing here?" I asked again.

He blinked. "Well, what are you doing here?"

"This is my Father's boat. We're on a trip together."

He nodded, accepting my response. "Are you having fun? With your father, I mean?"

I stared down at my wrapped hands. If I were being honest, I had never been so miserable in my life.

I laugh thinking back on that now. Back then I didn't even know misery. See, I know now that yes, sometimes things can get better, but things can also be worse. Much worse. After what I have been through, dealing with Father wouldn't be so bad.

At last, I admitted to Pan, "Not really."

His thin brows pinched together. His green eyes gazed at me, perplexed. "Then why are you still here?"

I shared in his confusion. "Well, where else would I go?"

His eyes brightened and his smile gleamed. "You could come with me."

"Where?"

He jumped off the bed into a standing position once again. "Why, to Neverland, of course!"

"Where is that?" I asked. "New Finland?"

His chest shook with laughter. "It's like no place you have ever been." He ran over to my side of the bed and took my hand in his, pulling me up to join him. Together, we ran up the steps and out onto the deck. He pointed at the stars. "It's out there. Beyond the farthest star your eyes can see."

I doubted him. Perhaps I was still dreaming after all. How else could a boy travel through space and amongst the stars? "How would we get there?"

His eyebrows danced. "With magic."

I shook my head. "I don't think so. There is no such thing as magic."

He sighed. Hands up, he admitted, "Okay, okay, you got me. It's not magic."

I let go of a breath I hadn't even realized I was holding. I felt deflated somehow. Even though I knew there was no such thing as magic, in the second I held my breath, I was hoping to be proven wrong.

He picked right back up where he'd left off with a shrug. "At least it's not human magic. It's fairy magic. Fairy dust to be exact. With it, we can do almost anything."

"Prove it," I demanded, still not convinced.

"As you wish." He winked at me and bowed. With his eyes closed and his palms facing up, he began to lift off the deck until he was floating above it.

I gasped. There was no way it was possible. I rubbed my fists over my eyes. When I looked at him again, he was still hovering in the air, hands outstretched. I was convinced.

"What do you say, James? Will you come with me to Neverland?"

I almost placed my hand in his when a thought struck me. "What about my father?"

His face remained soft and unfazed. "Do you really want to stay here with him?"

"No." I wrapped my fingers around his hand and once we were touching, my feet lifted off the ground as well. "Whoa," I breathed. I felt weightless.

"Are you ready?" I nodded as he pulled out his pocket watch. "Here we go!"

Pan hit the notch meant to open the face of the watch or to change the time. When he pressed the notch, we were lurched upwards into the sky, in the same direction he had pointed at when we were on the boat. It felt like we were flying through a dark tunnel, except all around us were stars, and planets, and galaxies, zooming by so fast I couldn't be sure if they were ever there.

The whole trip probably lasted a couple of minutes, but passed by like seconds. Before I could blink, we broke through the other end of the tunnel into a whole new world. Into Neverland.

We popped out of the bright blue sky and took aim at a forest below. I watched in horror as the yellow-green leaves that looked like fluffy green clouds a moment ago got closer and bigger, and I knew that underneath those leaves would be an entanglement of strong tree limbs ready to break our fall. I shielded my eyes with the crook of my arm.

Peter Pan laughed. I felt the wind change direction around us and wondered why we hadn't fallen to our deaths yet.

I dared to peak under my arm to see that we had changed course and were now flying just above the trees. I reached out my hand and brushed the leaves as we flew.

Excitement flooded me, and I found myself laughing. How many kids would ever have the chance to say he flew above the treetops and felt the tallest, brightest, and softest leaves in their hands? How many kids would get to say they knew what it felt like to feel the warm breeze bustle through their hair and clothes? I knew this was a special moment I would cherish forever. And I had one person to thank for it all.

Pan's bright eyes twinkled at me. "Are you ready to land now?"

I nodded. He pulled us forward, moving through the air around us even faster. He was searching for a specific place. He dived down in a small space between the trees and maneuvered us both around their spiraling limbs until we were a few inches from the ground.

Suddenly, he pulled back and did what looked like a half-somersault so his bare feet were the first part of his body to touch the ground. I tried to do the same, but somehow managed to fall on my butt instead.

He didn't laugh or scowl at me. Instead, he smiled down at me kindly and offered his hand. I let him pull me up and brushed off the back of my slacks. I looked around us. Neverland didn't seem so different from home. The forest reminded me of the trees I used to play in my own town. I was still breathing it all in when Pan called to me, "This way, James."

I followed him as he jumped and hopped through the thistle, making his way down a path he had obviously navigated many times. I wasn't as graceful as I stumbled after him, tripping over roots and getting caught in vines.

Pushing branches out of my way, I asked, "Where are we going?"

Without looking back, he replied, "To introduce you to the others."

Others? I wondered. There was a moment on the boat where I had felt special. Like Pan had picked me out for a reason. It was in this moment that I started to feel less unique. That sensation only grew when I did meet the others.

I was so focused on keeping my path clear and keeping myself from tripping over any more roots that I didn't notice when Pan stopped walking until I ran into his back. He stood stroking the dark brown trunk of an old tree.

"I'm home, old friend." Then he knelt to a hole in the trunk just big enough for us to crawl through. He howled into the hole and waited. A moment later, something howled back at him. He turned to face me with a grin. "Okay, they're down there. Let's go!"

He sat back into the dirt and slid forward, preparing to head into the hole legs first. "Meet you down there!" he called as he disappeared into the tree trunk, hollering and hooting the whole way.

I took a big breath, sucking in all the air I could as if it were confidence. Then I fell back on my butt and slid into the hole, feet first, as Peter had done. I held my breath as I fell underground, my butt sliding on a winding vine that had been hallowed out for this exact purpose, I presumed. The air thickened, the heat increasing, the further underground I went. For most of the ride, I fell through a dark, narrow dirt hole.

Suddenly, the tunnel opened wide and spat me out in a large room lit up with small glowing orbs that floated to the ceiling. I was flicked off the tongue of the root and fell onto the hard dirt floor with an oomph. I expected the air to be thick and humid as it had been in the tunnel, but when I inhaled my first breath since going through the hole, my lungs took in clean cool air. Pleasantly surprised, I continued to gulp in the air my chest was burning for.

Once I collected myself, I sat up. In front of me was a giant group of boys. The first thing I noticed, besides their tattered, worn clothing and the dirt on their faces, was that Peter and I were the oldest boys there. Peter knelt, his nose just mere centimeters from mine.

"Boys," he said, addressing the group behind him. He stood back up and gestured down to me with an open palm. "Welcome the newest member of our family!"

The boys behind him collectively cheered. His face came close to mine once again as he bent at the hips to meet me at my level. "And James, meet the Lost Boys."

I peered around Pan, taking in each boy behind him. I couldn't help but to fixate on their clothing, torn at some parts and patched in others. Some even had tears through their patches. How long had the boys been in Neverland? Were they from Neverland, like Pan, or were they from my world? I had so many questions to ask, but Peter swept me up and threw me into the crowd so fast I didn't get the chance to ask.

I bounced around the mob as every boy rushed to get a good look at me.

"Ey! He's an old one, Peter. Even for you!" one shouted.

"What is his job going to be?" asked another.

"Where are you from?" whispered a smaller boy, who wore a hat made from skunk fur.

Before I could answer, I was pushed around again. "What's his name?"

Pan shrugged. He wore a smile full of pride as he gazed upon his pack. "What should we name him?" he asked the boys.

30

"I-I have a name." I tried to speak above the uproar as the boys contemplated what to call me.

Peter grabbed my wrist and pulled me from the mob with ease. With a wave of his hand, he exclaimed, "Nonsense! Everyone gets a new name here."

"A new name?" I looked back at the boys with an uneasy feeling crawling in my stomach. Out of all these boys, none of their names were real? Again, I wondered how long they had been in Neverland, and I realized Pan had recruited each and every one of them. They all had families and lives outside of Neverland. Lives it looked like they had left a long time ago.

He laughed. "Of course. That's how you become one of us!"

"But my name is James."

His face flashed dark. It was so quick, so subtle, I thought my eyes were playing tricks on me. I thought the demons I had with my father had followed me to Neverland as well. I needed to learn to trust, I realized. Not everyone was going to harm me. Trust is a good thing. A great thing, even.

But trust in the wrong person could lead you down a path you never wanted to go, as it did for me. I chose to trust Peter Pan, and soon, I would begin to regret it.

He gave me a pat on the back and laughed. Addressing the group, he said, "The newbie is right, guys. He's only been with us for a few minutes. We shouldn't assign him a name right off the bat. We've got to get to know him first. Am I right?"

"Right!" They exclaimed in unison, punching the air with their fists.

CHAPTER THREE

Once the excitement died down, Peter introduced me to the Lost Boys one by one. Everything overwhelmed me, and I struggled to hold my attention on the tiny boy in front of me.

"This is Tootles," Peter joyfully shouted at me. "Now, Tootles is the unlucky one! He must have missed more adventures than I can count! But the best thing about him is that he never lets it get him down, isn't that right, Tootles!"

I watched the excitement grow on his little face as he nodded back at Peter. He was the youngest of the group, couldn't have been any older than six years old. He wore a hat made from skunk fur that seemed a little too big for his head. I could just about see his rosy cheeks and Bambi eyes. His clothes were almost identical to the other boys, the only thing separating them being the different animal fur they boasted.

Nibs was the next boy to be introduced. He was dressed like a rabbit and was described as the bravest of the bunch. He had wiry brown hair and, like most of the boys, was very thin. "Great to meet you! Peter hasn't recruited a new lost boy in forever! He must really have liked you!"

I met the remainder of the boys. The first was named Slightly, the oldest and the fox. The twins, who were an adorable pair of tiny raccoons, and finally Curly was a rather large boy who resembled a bear and described me as a pickle, although I still don't understand what that means.

I was instructed by Peter to go and rest. The boys were preparing a welcoming feast in honor of my arrival and mentioned something about an initiation. The idea was daunting. What if I failed? Would I have to go back to my father? No. That couldn't happen. I never wanted to see him again.

I was now in my bedroom. It was very small, though I didn't have to share like the other boys. There was no window, no door, just a small wooden bed that looked as if someone had already been using it for a long time.

It's not the end of the world, I thought. I could get used to this. I quickly curled up under the sheets and drifted off into what felt like an eternal slumber.

I wasn't sure how long I'd been asleep, but when I woke to the loud shouting and cheering of the other boys, I was feeling much better and more refreshed. Rolling onto my side, I found the twins standing there, silently staring at me. I don't know how long they'd been there, but they seemed to be pleased I was awake.

"Dinner's ready!" the first yelled.

"Get it while it's hot," followed the other.

Walking into the dining area, I marveled at the gigantic feast they had prepared. The food sprawled across the long table. Mountains of fruit and vegetables, meats and fish.

"Well, don't just stand there. Dig in," Peter said from across the room.

I sat down and piled up my plate. The food was incredible. I had never eaten anything so tasty in my entire life. I was in the middle of stuffing my mouth with roast potatoes when the initiation they mentioned earlier was brought back up.

"So! Let's get down to business. After you've eaten, it's time to become one of us."

"And how do I do that?" I asked between scoffing down more potatoes.

"By completing the initiation, of course! You'll get your new name and then finally be a lost boy like us."

I still wasn't fond of the idea of getting a new name. I liked being James and the idea of having a silly name didn't sit too well with me.

"Okay," I muttered. "I think I'm ready."

I wasn't really ready. I just didn't want to upset Peter.

We spent the rest of dinner talking about adventures. The boys had been on more than I could count. Tales of treasure, battles with dastardly pirates and, my personal favorite, the story of how Peter befriended a fairy named Tinkerbell. Peter found Tinkerbell alone and injured out in the middle of the forest. If it wasn't for Peter, she would have died, and because of this, he had a close bond with the fairies, who the boys said were the size of bugs.

Once everyone was done, Peter instructed them to go to bed and told me it was time for the initiation. I was foolish to ever think I had an idea of what was about to happen. This was the first time Peter was being his true self. Not the nice caring Peter he wanted me to believe he was but instead, a horrible manipulative Peter. The worst part of all, I didn't even know it was happening even though it was all right in front of my eyes the entire time. He was to trick me. Trick me into giving up my old life and old memories, so he would have full control.

We headed deep into the forest. Peter handed me a torch so I could see where I was going and told me to prepare for a long walk. As he handed me the glowing fire, I caught a glimpse of his face, half in shadow. His eyes flashed red and appeared to sink into his skin, while his smile was cruel. It was only an instant, but even now I look back on that moment and feel the chills running down my spine.

I followed Peter closely, making sure I didn't get lost in the labyrinth. The forest was thick with trees and plants, most of them unlike anything I had ever seen before. Some even seemed to be alive. This island was truly magical.

Strangely, we didn't speak to one another the entire time. The only sound came from the many animals inhabiting the forest and the crunching of branches and leaves beneath our feet. I felt more anxious with every step we took. I couldn't stop thinking about having to go back with my father. The memory of him hitting me replaying over and over in my head. The thought of facing his wrath after leaving without word made me slightly nauseous.

I was just about to ask Peter how much further we had to walk when he came to a sudden halt. I knocked into him. "Your challenge awaits you, James. Should you make it back out, you'll be one of us!"

I couldn't see where he was talking about. It was far too dark and he was too tall for me to see over. Stepping to the side, I made out what looked like a cave. The entrance was small but it seemed large enough for me to climb into. Taking a deep breath, I made my way toward the entrance. This was really it. It was time to say farewell to my old life and begin my new one.

"Good luck! I know you can do this, James. I believe in you!" Those were the last words Peter said to me before I left him behind and crawled into the cave.

The cave itself was gigantic inside. I was able to stand with plenty of room. It was far from claustrophobic, which settled the anxious feeling in my stomach. Looking around, I couldn't see anything that seemed out of place or that could be tied to a challenge. It was completely empty. Water dripped from the ceiling, dampening the rocks and soil, giving off a rich smell of earth.

Making my way forward, I walked into the center of the cave, scanning the room for anything that could help me. That's when it happened. To this day, I'm still not totally aware how Pan was able to do what he did. The traveling to Neverland was one thing but this was something else entirely. There, before my very eyes, was my father. I was only able to see him from behind and never managed to pluck up the courage to see him face-to-face but it was him. I know it was.

"James!" My name bellowed through the room, echoing over and over. "How dare you abandon me. What kind of a son does that to their own father?"

I stood still with shock. The only words I managed to stutter out of my mouth never even made any sense. I was in a state of panic. My worst fear had come true; my father was here. He'd come to take me away.

"I..I.. I'm not coming back with you," I finally managed to blurt out.

"You will come with me immediately or not at all. I haven't got time for you and your childish behavior. How do you ever expect to become a man living here where you'll remain a child for eternity?"

For a split second, he almost made me think twice about why I was here, but the anger and hatred I had toward him made me dismiss it.

"I'm staying here. If becoming a man means ending up like you, I will never leave." I had never stood up to my father like this before. Knowing I had to see him every day on that ship stopped me from ever doing such a thing.

"If that's your final decision, then consider yourself orphaned. I won't have such a pathetic excuse for a son in my life. Now go! I want you gone."

My feet were moving before I had even realized it, and before I knew it, I was back out in the forest, running as fast as my feet would let me. Ignoring Peter, I made my way deeper into the forest. My thoughts were racing a mile a minute with tears dripping down my face. Finally coming to a stop, I stood crying as I waited for Peter to catch up. Tears blurred my vision. My feet ached. And my heart was uncomfortably in my throat.

"James. James!" I could hear Peter calling out for me. I ignored his calls, not wanting to move. When he finally found me, Peter didn't say a word. Instead, he opened his arms and took me in for a hug. "You did it, James. You're one of us," he whispered.

After making sure I was okay, Peter took me back to the treehouse so we could tell the others the news. I was expecting everyone to be asleep but to my surprise, they were all eagerly waiting for our arrival.

"One of us! One of us!" they cheered.

"Peter, does he get a new name now?" Slightly asks.

"What's his name? What's his name?" Tootles roars.

"I'm gonna call him Ace. Yeah, Ace."

The boys went into an uproar. "Ace! Ace! Ace!" they continued to cheer. Ace wasn't too bad of a name. I was starting to like it. I felt wanted here, like I belonged. Ace, it was.

I was next handed my new clothes. They were exactly like the rest of the boys, just not as ruined and my animal fur was from a wolf. I noticed something this time, though. Two boys who I didn't get introduced to the first time. Like mine, their clothes looked brand new, and they just sat in the corner away from everybody, talking between themselves. I wanted to ask who they were but knew I wouldn't get the chance just yet.

I got changed and went back to join the group. They wanted to throw a party to celebrate me becoming a lost boy. I'd not even been there a day and they had already welcomed me into the family, threw me a feast and now a party. Peter really did know how to lure people in. The remainder of the evening was the best memory of Pan I have. This was the first time I got to fly. Call me crazy, but it really did happen.

After blowing some fairy dust in my face, I felt the same weightless as before. Looking down, I watched my body leave the ground. I was surprisingly not afraid and instead embraced the magic. Higher and higher we flew, eventually being above the clouds.

Taking my hand, Peter led me on a journey I will never forget. We flew over the entire island, everything below looking like tiny ants. I never wanted it to stop and when it did come to an end, I craved that feeling of excitement again.

We all headed off to sleep soon after. I didn't want to sleep. I just wanted to spend more time with Peter and the lost boys. Sleep meant time to myself and that would only lead to thinking about the encounter with my father.

I had a nightmare that night. One about the cave. This time my father did take me away and forced me to spend the rest of my life on that ship, cleaning it over and over, getting hit over and over.

I shot up, breathing heavy, covered in cold sweat. I needed to find Pan. He would help me.

I tiptoed my way into his bedroom, making sure to be quiet. To my surprise, Peter wasn't in his bed or nowhere to be seen. I decided to go looking for him out in the forest. So, grabbing a torch and a blanket, I set off in search of him.

I was careful not to go too far and after ten minutes, I turned around to return. The moon and stars shone so much brighter than I'd ever seen before. They lit up the whole island like a second sun. I noticed something strange with the stars that night. The star constellations were not familiar at all. How was that possible? Maybe I was just tired.

The next morning, I was told I was going to be assigned a job like everyone else. These were simple things, like mining for fairy dust, foraging food and collecting materials. My job was a little harder than that. Peter had an old ship he wanted to restore. He also wanted me to teach him how to sail. I happily accepted. The more time with Peter, the better. Later that day, he took me down to the beach and there in the bay was a small beaten up ship. It was going to take a lot of hard work and time, but I was ready to take on the challenge.

"Let's get to work, shall we? This ship won't fix itself," I said to Pan, patting him on the back.

CHAPTER FOUR

Months passed. The ship was starting to really come together. All of the wood work was completed and the ship now had sails. A few more finishing touches and it would be ready to set sail.

I was proud of what we had accomplished. Peter was a real help. Every morning after breakfast, the two of us would come down to the beach and get to work. Some days we would work without breaks, to ensure the job was done as quickly as possible. Peter scavenged any materials I asked for and even got ahold of some paint so that we could design a flag for the ship.

The only thing troubling me was the fact that every night, without fail, Peter would disappear. On a few occasions, I nearly confronted him about it but would always stop myself. I supposed if he wanted me to know where he was going, he would have told me.

Still, after all this time, I was itching to find out the truth so one night I decided to stay up and follow him. I wanted to get to the bottom of this.

I waited for hours and hours but eventually, Peter got up and left. I soon followed, making sure he wasn't aware, sticking to the shadows with every twist and turn. He was headed for the beach. The moonlight lit up the sea and it shone like the glossiest crystals. It was a beautiful sight to behold.

Reaching into his breast pocket, Pan pulled out a small golden stopwatch. What I can only describe as a portal of some kind appeared above the moist white sand. After he stepped into it, it collapsed on itself and vanished into thin air, taking Peter with it.

I rubbed my eyes for several seconds to make sure I had really seen what I thought I did. Where was Pan going? He hadn't brought back more lost boys so that couldn't have been it. This was very suspicious. There must be a reason for it that no one knows. Something wasn't right here. Maybe coming here was a big mistake.

Using this as a prime opportunity, I rushed back to the tree house to grab my constellation book. I looked up at the sky and started to read the stars.

I knew it! Flicking page after page, I couldn't match a single one. We were not on earth. At least if we were, we were nowhere anyone has ever been before. I had to confront Peter. I needed to get the truth once and for all. Is this what Peter wanted, to hide us away from the rest of the world?

Not knowing how much time I had left until Peter would return, I hurried back to bed and headed straight to sleep. Tomorrow, on the boat, I would speak to Peter.

I scarfed down breakfast as fast as I could, said my good mornings and raced off to the ship. I needed to prepare myself for the confrontation. When Peter eventually arrived, we carried on with work as normal. I was waiting for the perfect opportunity. One where he had no choice but to confess.

"I'm going to do another run for supplies. Anything you need, Ace? I'll be sure to get it."

This was my chance. Taking a big gulp, I chose my words carefully. "Actually, yes. There is something I need. I noticed you disappear every night. Where do you go? And also, I've noticed that the star constellations don't match any I have ever read about. Where are we exactly?"

Peters face switched almost instantly. His eyes filling with anger. This wasn't the same Peter I knew and loved. This was a different person entirely. The one I had caught a glimpse of the night of initiation.

"Are you a lost boy?" he screamed at me.

I was frozen still. Unsure of what to say, I slowly nodded my head in shame.

"Yes. You are! Well, lost boys don't ask these ridiculous questions. You are on Neverland and what I do in my spare time is none of your concern. Do you understand me?"

I understood perfectly. I wanted out. My suspicions were right. This was all too good to be true. Something was going on. To avoid angering Peter further, I apologized and promised not to speak of such things anymore. Peter decided not to go and get supplies and instead assisted me with building living quarters on the ship.

It was very hot that day. The sun beamed down, the little breeze still as hot as fire. I wanted to take a rest, hydrate myself with water and continue on when it was cooler. I finished the task I was doing and sat down in the shade of the trees. Peter came and joined me, and we exchanged some small chit chat while sipping out of coconuts.

"I've got something important I have to attend to. I won't be back until tomorrow so I need you to be in charge. Think you can do that for me, Ace?"

Even after his earlier outburst, I was flattered that he wanted to appoint me temporary leader of the lost boys during his absence. I saw this as an opportunity to speak to the boys about Peter's disappearances and the idea of leaving, so I quickly took him up on the offer.

"Of course, it would be my pleasure. I'll make the boys continue with their work and will make sure they go to sleep at the usual time," I responded.

He smiled, ruffled my hair and then left. "Thank you, Ace. I'll see you very soon."

Once he'd left, I sat in the shade for a little while longer, then finished up my work on the boat. I informed the boys of Peters absence and explained how I would be in charge. Slightly didn't seem too pleased, claiming he was usually the one in charge, but I just ignored it and carried on as normal.

Once dinner was finished, I dismissed the boys and allowed them to spend the rest of their day doing whatever they pleased. This was my golden opportunity to start figuring a way off the island, as well as getting some dirt on Peter. Knowing that Slightly was the best person to help me, I asked him to give me a tour of the island. If there was any chance of escaping, I needed to have a proper map of the environment. It would have been at a great disadvantage not knowing where I was going. It would be very easy to get lost.

I grabbed a few essentials, such as food and water and, of course, paper and some pencils. The island was pretty large from what I remember. The time in the air, although short, really did show me the size of our home. The island itself did hold some very beautiful locations. There were the Scarlet falls, a mammoth-sized waterfall with an underground cave system home to the mermaids. Several forests and even jungles inhabited by creatures said to only live here. I didn't see many, although I did spot what I could only describe as a fox with scales and spikes. Slightly said this was called a Clarizfan. Funny name for a not-so-funny-looking creature.

The tour was starting to come to an end and I still hadn't mentioned anything to Slightly about Peter so before we got back, I made sure to ask. "Slightly, there's something I want to ask and I was wondering if you could help me."

"Of course, Ace. Anything for you"

"I noticed Peter goes away every night. Sometimes he doesn't come back for hours. Where is it that he goes and why does he do it?"

Slightly paused for a second and then answered, "That's when Peter goes to find new lost boys. He's very picky with who he brings back and that's why we have not seen anyone return since you came along."

"Why does he do that?" I asked.

"Here on Neverland, you never grow up. You stay a kid forever and ever. He wants us to stay here with him and have an everlasting friendship."

Suddenly, it all made sense. He was bringing us here to work for him. To do all the jobs he couldn't do alone. At the time, I didn't understand why he was doing this, but I was no longer going to be fooled.

"But what about if I wanted to leave, would he take me home?"

Slightly quickly interrupted me. "Nobody leaves. It's against the rules of being a lost boy to do so. Besides, why would you ever want to leave? Being a kid forever will be awesome. Grownups are boring and horrible."

Not wanting to cause a dispute, I left the conversation at that and asked to be taken back to the treehouse. I instructed everyone to go to bed a little earlier that night. I needed to map the stars next. I had no idea how long that was going to take and couldn't risk the boys finding out.

I already worried about Slightly informing Peter of our earlier discussions. Taking a compass from Peter's room, I started my quest. I mapped ten new constellations that night and concluded that heading north would be my best bet.

I was really doing this. I was really plotting my way off Neverland.

CHAPTER FIVE

When I woke up the next morning, I had come up with the perfect plan. I had decided Pan and I would finish the ship. That way, I could gain his complete trust. And when it was finished, I could jump aboard the ship and sail away at night when Pan disappeared through his portal in search of another lost boy. It seemed brilliant at the time, and I remember feeling very proud of myself.

I quickly devoured my breakfast once again, anticipating the start of the day. Today, Pan and I were working on the ship's wheel. Once we finished the wheel, we only had a few days left until the ship would be completed. And then I would be free from the evil Pan really was. I just wished I had figured it out before I decided to leave Father.

"Come on, Ace!" Peter called from the other end of the table, snapping me out of my thoughts as fast as lightning. "We're almost done with the ship! We should get started for the day. Come on, everyone! Time to begin our daily work."

The twins excitedly jumped from the table, shoving one more piece of fruit into their mouths before skipping away together. I grabbed my bag of tools and walked through the forest with Pan, to the beach where we were building the ship.

"Can you keep a secret, Ace?"

I hadn't expected that. Here I was, some lonely boy who had fallen for his tricks, and yet he wanted to tell me a secret? Was this a trick, or had I already gained that much of his trust?

"Of course, I can. I have kept many secrets before," I stated. Which was kind of true. I had kept many secrets from my parents, like most boys. But I wanted Pan to trust me as much as possible before I could escape.

"I've always wanted to sail somewhere," he said. His face crinkled a little, almost in disappointment. "But I haven't because I've never learned how to swim. I could probably use Fairy Dust to fly back but that would be a waste because it's not that easy to get."

I can teach him to swim, I thought. That would surely gain his trust. We could practice a little every day when we worked on the boat and by the time, it was ready he should be able to swim. So, I had told him my plan and he quickly agreed. He made me promise to keep it a secret from the rest of the group because he wanted to surprise them with it. For whatever reason, I didn't know. I still don't to this day.

***

Two days later, we were waist deep in the surprisingly warm waters of what I had assumed was an ocean at the time. It was as clear as the sky that day. Small waves lapped at the spongy shore.

51

"Okay, so when you're underwater, you can open your eyes or leave them closed. I like to have mine open, but it bothers some people. And you have to try not to hold your nose this time. Otherwise, you will have to swim one handed, which I don't think will work very well." I giggled.

Although I knew Pan was a bad person, teaching him to swim was kind of nice. It felt good because I knew something he didn't. I was going to escape, and he had no idea.

"Like this?" He took a deep breath and splashed under the surface of the clear water, pushing forward with his hands out in front and his feet kicking quickly behind. He was a fast learner, a trait he had probably perfected throughout the years.

"Very good!" I yelled as soon as he appeared above water again. "If I didn't know any better, I would think you knew how to swim all along."

"Right," he agreed. "I bet I could even swim faster than you, Ace." A cocky smile spread across his face while his eyes met mine in challenge. I knew he wanted to beat me to prove he was the leader, but I also knew there was no way he would win. I had been swimming for years.

"How about we race to the ship?" I offered. It was sitting by the edge of the water about 300 feet from where we were. "If you win, I will teach you to sail." I figured even if I did lose, I wouldn't be around to teach him anyway.

Pan's eyes flared with excitement, something I had rarely seen.

"Okay, and if you win, I will let you hold my watch." The hairs on my arms stood on end. I was surprised he had known that was something I wanted. If I could get him to let me hold it, maybe I could get him to tell me how it worked.

"Deal," I hastily agreed.

As soon as we both took off, I knew he didn't stand a chance. I kicked my feet as hard as I could, thinking about home and how hard I would hug Mum and Father once I got there. I pushed with everything I had until I reached the shore.

Looking behind me to see how close Pan was, I realized I couldn't even see where he was. I searched the water frantically until I spotted him throwing his arms above his head and gasping for air.

"Pan!" I screamed.

"Help! Ace! I can't—" he gasped. But I didn't hear the rest as I dove back into the water and swam to him as fast as possible. Sure, he was a bad guy, but that didn't mean I would just let him die. Although, looking back, maybe I should have.

I grabbed him by the shoulders and swam for the shore. As we neared the beach, I dragged him onto the sand and laid him on his back so that he could catch his breath. He coughed up water between pants.

"Thank you," cough, "Ace," he said weakly. "You saved my life."

A few minutes later, Pan climbed to his feet and stared somberly at the water's edge.

"Can you keep another secret?" he asked. "This one's pretty important."

I nodded, not knowing what to say at the time. Little did I know, his next words would forever change the course of my life. For better or worse, I'm not sure. I suppose that's for you to decide.

Pan pulled his watch from the ship's bow. "You saw me leave Neverland the other night, didn't you?"

I stayed silent. I wasn't sure if I should be scared or surprised. My body didn't know what to do, so silence was the best option.

"It's powered by Starstuff," he confessed. "It allows me to leave Neverland so that I can search for lost boys like you and save them. It's very hard to find, you see."

"What is it made from?" I asked. I walked closer, to get a better look at it.

"It comes from stars that are wished upon by all the unhappy children. It's how I found you, Ace." Pan turned to me, a small smile on his face. "It lets me do anything I want. I can control the plants and animals on Neverland if I choose, and I can travel wherever I want to find boys like you." A dark emotion crossed Pan's face in that moment. A flash of what he really was, which he kept hidden well most of the time. But every occasionally, I would catch it. "I have to save as many as I can, Ace. It's what I do."

I realized then that I had to change my plan. I couldn't just leave all of the other lost boys here on Neverland. I had to steal the watch. It was the only way I could save everyone and make sure that Pan would be trapped here forever. He wouldn't be able to steal anyone else ever again.

***

Later that night, Peter got ready for his nightly quest outside of Neverland as usual.

This is perfect, I thought. I could steal the watch when he got back because he went straight to sleep. I got everything ready as soon as I noticed he was gone. I was going to finally do this.

But when Pan returned, he wasn't alone. Beside him stood a stocky white-haired boy with a red hat on. His little eyes darted back and forth, taking in everything around him.

"This is Smee, everyone!" Pan announced. "Smee, this is Nibs, Slightly, Cubby, and Tootles." The twins had already gone to bed so he didn't bother introducing them. They all nodded except for Cubby. He waddled over to Smee in his bear outfit and gave him a small hug.

"Hi, Smee," he said.

Pan then looked at me and pushed Smee until he stood right next to me. "And this, dear one, is Ace. You can sleep next to Ace until morning. He can help you with anything you will need."

Great, I thought. Now I couldn't steal his watch.

I felt a great amount of disappointment as Smee and I settled down for bed. He kept tossing and turning, clearly uncomfortable and not willing to sleep so I decided I would see what brought him here.

"Are you okay?" I asked. I rolled onto my side so that we could talk freely.

Smee turned to me, wrapped in his small blanket. "I... don't know," he whispered. "I wanted to come here more than anything in the world, but something doesn't feel right." His eyebrows dropped low on his eyes, his mouth twisting to the side like he was deep in thought. "But I have nowhere else to go," he confessed.

Taking a deep breath, I told Smee everything I knew. It was probably the best decision I made that day, looking back now. Smee would prove to be a very valuable person and one of my best friends.

"So, you see, I have to steal that watch so I can get all of us out of here. We can work together and find somewhere safe. But this isn't where we need to be. We need to get out of here as fast as we can. I don't know what he's planning to do with us, but I have this strange feeling that it isn't good at all. There are moments when I see pure evil in him. I can't really explain it, but it isn't good, Smee. I don't know what else to do."

He excitedly sat up on his makeshift bed. "I can take it for you, Ace! I'm a very good thief, at least where I come from. I can steal anything without getting caught!" It was the first time I had seen him smile since he arrived. I couldn't help but believe him.

"Okay, Smee," I said with a smile. "Show me what you got."

Minutes later, he returned, quietly tiptoeing toward his bed. "I got it!" A mischievous smile spread across his lips, a small twinkle gleaming in his eyes. I couldn't believe it.

"We have to make sure it works," I whispered. "Come on, let's go."

Smee quickly agreed and as we made our way through the forest minutes later, I felt like I was floating all over again. If we could make this watch work, I could go home. We could all go home. I had already decided that Smee would come with me. He had nowhere to go, and I might not either. After all, Father had told me he never wanted to see me again.

Shaking my head at the possibility, I heard a deep menacing scream coming from a couple hundred feet away. The whole forest went quiet, and it felt like time stood still. Pan had woken up, and judging from the ground-shaking roar, he had figured out his watch was gone.

"Run!" I screamed. "We have to make it to the beach!"

Smee's eyes grew wide like saucers, registering the fear laced in my voice. Immediately, we ran as fast as our feet could carry us. Jumping over vines and roots below, and dodging leaves and branches above, we weaved our way through the forest with Pan close behind.

As soon as our feet hit the sand, I pulled the watch from my pocket, clicking it open. It gleamed in the darkness as a powerful sensation crept through me.

"How does it work?" Smee screamed frantically, looking back toward the forest behind us. We both knew Pan would be flying toward us any minute. We were running out of time.

"When I saw him use it, he just pressed this part," I nervously said as I slammed my thumb onto the watches edge. *Click.*

My heart dropped as nothing happened, our worst fears coming true. *Click, click.* But no matter how hard I pressed it, nothing was happening.

"I don't understand," I screamed, puzzled. I ran toward the boat, Smee following close behind. I was grasping at straws now, hoping it would work once we got to the ship.

Just as our feet hit the deck, a loud noise slammed us both to the ground. I thought it was thunder, but no storms came to Neverland. At least that's what I had been told.

"Traitor!" Pan screamed, slamming his sword against the wooden deck. I glanced up, noticing Pan's hair looking strange as could be. It was standing straight up, like electricity was moving it. I felt static in the air as I grappled for a way to escape.

"I told everyone what you did, Ace." Pan's eyes grew menacing, as his true form appeared in front of me once again. "They all know you are the one taking magic from this island." His smile grew, like a wild animal baring its teeth before a kill.

As he stepped toward us, my hand grew warm. I looked down to see that the watch had started to glow as bright as a star. *Tick, tick, tick.* Confused and distracted, I didn't notice Pan stepping closer until Smee grabbed my other arm.

The watch grew brighter and brighter with each step Pan took. My only thought was to get as far away from him as we could.

"We have to go," I whispered to Smee.

We both made a run for the front of the ship. Even if we had to swim, we were going to make it out of here. I made a promise to Smee, and I was going to keep it.

"No!" Pan bellowed, taking a giant leap toward us both. "You ruined everything! I should have killed you when I had the chance, James. You will never escape this. Give me my watch, and I promise to let Smee live."

I turned to Smee, thinking that if I couldn't make it out alive, at least he would. We were now standing at the edge of the ship, the crystal cool water dancing below. There was nowhere to go.

The watch gripped tight in my left hand was a ball of light, vibrating my whole body. There was no time to think. I had to do something.

"Your time is up, James. Now you must die," came Pan's booming voice as he sprinted toward us, sword in hand.

Giving it one last shot, I locked arms with Smee, an attempt to catapult us overboard. All I could see was the anger and evil radiating from Pan's dark eyes. I had never seen them so black before.

As we tipped backward, his sword took aim in one final attempt to reach me. I moved my right hand out to block the blow, not realizing I was pressing the clock down with my left.

Just as I realized I was about to die, a portal appeared just above the water. An incredible amount of pressure pulled us toward the entrance. In those last seconds before Smee and I escaped, I locked eyes with Pan.

"Nooo!" he screamed as he sliced his sword toward me once again. I watched in horror as his blade sliced through the flesh of my right hand, cutting it clean off.

But before I could even register the pain, we were sucked into the portal and away from Pan once again.

CHAPTER SIX

The ground is very cold. That was my first thought after being sucked out of Neverland away from Pan. I didn't want to open my eyes because I was sure I was bleeding to death wherever we were.

I knew I was missing my hand, but I still couldn't feel any pain. I had to be in shock, bleeding out all over someone's floor somewhere. That was the only explanation I could think of at the time.

I sighed, my breath echoing in the dark room.

"Ace?" Smee's quiet voice whispered a few feet away.

"You can call me James, Smee. Pan gave me that name and I never want to hear it again." I sat up slowly, deciding I had better look at the wound while still conscious. That and I needed to figure out where we were.

"James." He seemed to ponder this. After a few seconds of silence, he continued. "Did... did he cut off your hand? Or was I hallucinating? Because nothing like this has ever happened to me and I'm not sure what to think."

Despite the situation, I had to smile. I was beginning to really like Smee and I kind of felt bad that he would soon be on his own. But as I looked down, my eyes adjusting to the dark light, I realized there was no blood at all. In fact, the wound seemed to be completely cauterized.

How is that possible? I wondered. Did the portal heal my wound? Was this the magic of Starstuff? I had no idea at the time, but Starstuff would turn out to be one of the most powerful substances in the world. *Worlds*, I should say. But that's further ahead.

"It seems as though he did, Smee. But I'm fine, there is no need to worry." I held up my arm for him to inspect. "At least we made it out alive. And with the watch, no less!"

Smee continued to stare at my forgotten hand, no doubt trying to process everything that had just happened. I stood up quickly, taking in my surroundings. There was a set of stairs directly to our left, leading up to a small door above. An end table sat next to the staircase, a newspaper resting on a corner. There were no windows, so I assumed it was a basement of some kind.

I quietly walked to the table and scooped what looked like a newspaper into my only hand.

"The third day of January, year 2017," I read aloud. But how could that be? We had made it back to London, as I could see the tower rising above all else from the basement window, but we were clearly years ahead.

Smee, realizing where we were, raced his small frame up the rickety stairs toward the small door.

"We need to get out of here," he stated. But when his hand settled on the knob, twisting back and forth, nothing happened.

"Locked."

I carried myself up the stairs to meet him. Maybe there was somebody inside that would hear us and let us free.

"Help!" I screamed. "Is anyone there? Help us!"

I frantically knocked on the door in hopes that someone would come to let us out. But there wasn't anything but silence. We continued pounding on the door for hours, exhausting ourselves until we both fell asleep leaning against the door, sitting on the top step.

"James, wake up!" Smee whispered, shaking my arm until I came to. "Someone is coming."

We both stood up, standing back as footsteps pounded closer and closer to the door. Just as they stopped, the door swung open, revealing a tall brown haired man. He was dressed head to toe in black, his thick rubber boots tapping the ground in frustration. That was when I realized he had what looked like a gun in his hand.

"What are you doing in my house?" the man cautiously asked, the gun firmly gripped at his side. He stared at our tattered clothes and dirty bodies, undoubtedly thinking we were some kind of thieves. I couldn't open my mouth because I didn't know how to explain everything that had happened.

"I said, what are you doing in my house?" he demanded. He raised his gun, taking aim at Smee who was frozen in fear.

"Wait, we can explain. sir! Please, just put the gun down. We aren't here to take anything and we don't mean to cause you any harm." I raised my arms above my head, showing the strange man that we were unarmed. Smee took notice and quickly did the same.

The man's dark eyes glanced over at Smee and quickly back to me. They lingered on my missing hand, something I would eventually have to get used to, before locking onto Pan's watch in my other.

"That watch, how did you get that?" he demanded. He looked as though he had seen it before, and a strange sensation crept up my arm.

"Have… have you seen it before?" I stuttered. "If you put the gun down, we'll tell you everything. Please." I locked eyes with the man once again, trying to calm him down and assess the situation at the same time.

Slowly, he lowered the gun, his eyes locked on the watch the entire time. A flash of pain crossed his face, quickly replaced by anger.

"My name is James, and this is Smee." I pointed next to me. "I know how this is going to sound but this watch threw us into your basement. We were trying to escape a very bad man and we had no other choice."

"Pan," the man whispered. He stepped aside and ushered us through the door. "Come, tell me everything."

***

The man's name was Hanzel. He had recognized the watch immediately when I held it up and I couldn't blame him for his reaction.

Many years ago, Hanzel had met Pan in a nightmare of his own. He and his sister, Gretel, were in search of a better life. They had been living in a terrible foster home together when Pan had taken them under his wing, wooing them with impossible dreams and happiness galore. He would visit them every night, promising them a better life. Anything was better than there.

But Pan quickly grew jealous of Gretel. "He would make her go to bed early sometimes when he told us stories, instead just telling them to me," Hanzel said. "I didn't think anything of it at first." He paused. "But I guess I should have."

He went on to explain that eventually Pan grew very angry at them both and would lash out at any inconvenience.

"Finally, one night, I returned from the bathroom to find my sister bloody and unconscious in our room. I knew Pan had done it but nobody would believe me. The foster home accused me of her murder, and the court obviously believed them over me. I was just an angry foster boy." He took a deep breath, rubbing his face with one of his rough hands. "I spent 6 years in juvenile detention, locked away from the world until I turned 21. Every day I vowed to avenge her death and find Pan when I got out."

Hanzel's face grew somber. "So, I will do whatever I can to help. I can protect you. I'm a bounty hunter now. It was the quickest way to gain the skills I needed. I have weapons, training, and skills you will need to stay safe. Pan must be stopped, lads. Not only to avenge my sister, but to protect everyone else he might harm."

"I agree," I said. "But we'll need more help." We couldn't do it on our own. Pan had already proven to be a very worthy opponent, and I was now at a very serious disadvantage.

"There are other watches, like Pan's. I've done a lot of research and know their basics, but we'll need to find them to defeat Pan once and for all." Hanzel stood up and walked to a dresser in the sitting room. Opening it, he revealed what seemed to be the same watch as Pan's.

"I also suggest that you get Pan's watch replicated, just as I have," Hanzel said as he walked back to Smee and me. I was amazed that you couldn't tell the difference between the two. "That way, when you eventually come into contact with him, you can trick him into thinking the copy is his. I know a place, if you like. It'll only take a few days. I can take you there tomorrow."

I stood up, glancing at Smee who was already asleep on the couch. "That would be great. I think we'll head to bed now, Hanzel. I can't thank you enough for letting us stay here until then. We really appreciate your help." I shook his hand, tucking the watch into my back pocket.

"It really is my pleasure, James." His face hardened, no doubt thinking about his sister Gretel. He wanted Pan stopped, even if it cost him his own life. It was written all over his face. "Goodnight," he said and left the room.

***

Two days later, the watch was finished. Hanzel had taken us to an amazing place that he had called a mall. There were so many shops, my head was spinning by the end of our journey. We made it back to his house and Smee was in a daze, begging to just lie down for a while.

I climbed into my makeshift bed on the floor of Hanzel's guestroom. I let Smee take the bed, his tiny frame surprisingly taking up a lot of room. As I closed my eyes, I couldn't help but think of my last encounter with Pan.

And as I drifted off, I was sucked into another nightmare of my own. I hadn't had a nightmare since I was with Father, but this one was much worse.

"Traitor!" Pan screamed. "I will kill you for this!"

He stood on the side of the ship, gripping his sword in one hand and one of the sail's in the other. He looked even more terrifying than I remember. Lightning flashed behind him, illuminating his livid face. Dark veins seemed to pop out of his forehead, his teeth gleaming and sharp when he spoke.

I was lying on the ship's deck, Smee nowhere to be found. I couldn't get up. My body wouldn't work as I struggled to get away. It felt like I was tied down to something, but my arms were free.

"Well, well, well, Ace." Pan's eyes turned black as he knelt beside me. His sword stroked my left cheek, scraping along the skin. "I knew I would find you. It was only a matter of time."

But how was that possible? He was trapped in Neverland. I had the watch. There was no way he could escape.

I gasped as a sat up as fast as I could, the nightmare fogging my brain. It had seemed so real. I rubbed my eyes, wiping away my tiredness. I couldn't go back to sleep after that.

Out of the corner of my eye, I noticed something glow. As my eyes adjusted, I realized what it was. The watch!

"Smee!" I yelled. "Wake up! We have to go!"

I couldn't believe it. Had Pan found me in my dreams? How did he know we would end up at Hanzel's so fast?

I shook Smee awake, practically dragging him into Hanzel's room with me. "We have to go! Hanzel, get ready!"

Hanzel flew out of bed, grabbing the gun he kept in his nightstand. "What happened?" he asked.

"The watch is glowing. Pan found me in my dreams. We have to leave as soon as possible." I looked frantically at him and Smee. Smee took a deep breath, realizing the gravity of the situation. We didn't think he could leave Neverland, but we had to find somewhere else to go just in case. If he found more Starstuff, who knew what he would be capable of.

We all gathered our things as fast as we could and met in the sitting room. I grabbed the watch from my pocket, which began to glow brighter and brighter as I opened it.

Click. I quickly pressed the button. We were immediately sucked into the portal, darkness rapidly replaced with flying stars and galaxies. It all went by so fast I didn't even have time to think about where we were going. Where would the watch take us this time?

Just as fast as we had entered the portal, we shot out onto a pile of sand. A beach? I stood up, dusting myself off. Hanzel had given us new clothes before we had left. What he called jeans and a t-shirt. I didn't really care what I looked like. Clothes were clothes as far as I was concerned. Although, it was much more comfortable than what Pan had given us.

"It looks like we're on another island," came Smee's voice. "It's not Neverland though. Look over there, James. It's where they dock ships." Smee pointed behind me, and as I turned around, I realized he was right.

Where are we? When are we? I thought.

"It looks to be a little bit of a walk to the docks, lads. Why don't we find a place to call home for the night up ahead?" Hanzel grabbed his pack and began walking in the direction of the docks. Smee and I quickly followed. If anyone knew how to make a home outside, it was him.

I tucked the watch back into my pocket, its glow subdued for the time being. "We should be able to stay here for a while. We need to figure out how we're going to find the rest of the watches if we have any chance at defeating Pan. He's already proven he can enter my dreams. We don't know what else he's capable of," I said to the group.

I didn't like the idea of that, and based on the looks Smee and Hanzel had on their faces, they didn't either.

As we made our beds for the night under a big, flat leafed tree, Smee tugged on the sleeve of my shirt. "James, we're going to need a lot of things. How are we going to do that?" His eyes were big and round, afraid we had already lost the battle.

"He's right," Hanzel agreed. "We're going to need money. We need food, shelter, more weapons, and more people than just us."

"We need a crew," I thought aloud. "Tomorrow, we'll find a ship and persuade the Captain into letting us work for him. I know a lot about boats. It should be easy!" I boasted. "We can save our money and get everything we need without being stuck in one place."

It's our only chance, I thought.

"Tomorrow it's," Hanzel said. "It's as good of a plan as any."

Smee smiled, lying down by me. "I've always wanted to be a pirate," he confessed. "I have a feeling this is a good plan, James." He yawned, stretching his limbs as far out as he could. "A very good plan."

I smiled back, feeling proud of myself. It would be hard work, but we had to do whatever we could to stop Pan.

***

The following morning, we embarked on our first journey in this new land. It seemed we were hundreds of years from where we had met Hanzel.

It only took us a few hours to find a ship with a captain on board. We got lucky because they were loading it full of supplies, getting ready to set sail.

"So, ye want to come aboard this here ship, do ye?" bellowed the captain's voice. He was a very tall man, his face covered with a thick black beard that went past his shoulders. He had on a big captain's hat and a red sash tied around his middle.

Well, Smee would be happy. He did say he wanted to be a pirate, I laughed to myself.

"Yes, sir. I know a lot about ships and so do my friends here," I lied. "We would be of good use to you. You won't regret it." I stood as tall as I could, Smee doing just the same while Hanzel leaned against the ship's rail.

"Stop with yer gibberish, boy. I'll have to pay you less than the rest of the crew. You have to start somewhere, you see." The captain smiled. One of his gold teeth gleamed in the sun. "And you'll have to work longer, too."

"That's not a problem, sir. I can help navigate at night, if you would like. I can guide us with the stars." I had hoped nobody else on the ship could do the same.

"Is that so, boy?" The captain slowly walked toward me again, a small smile on his face. "And what happened to yer hand?" he asked as his eyes laid upon my missing hand.

"Sword fight, sir." *Keep it simple*, I thought. That's all he needed to know.

"Well, you will need to use both of ye hands to work on this ship boy," said the captain. He motioned for one of his crew to come over. He was a short man with no hair and an eye patch over his left eye.

"Make him a hand, Tiny," he told the short man.

"Aye, aye, Captain," came Tiny's response.

I watched as Tiny grabbed a hook off the ship's deck, as well as a few other things and disappeared behind a sail.

Confused, I turned to Smee. What was he doing?

"And call me Blackbeard, boy!" The captain laughed, slapping me on the back.

"Blackbeard," I repeated as Tiny came strolling back toward the captain.

In his hand was a small contraption with a hook on one end and a hole in the other. Blackbeard quickly took the hook and grabbed my arm.

"Welcome aboard, boys," he said as he placed the hook over the stump on my right hand. "Time to show me what ye got... Hook." He winked.

By now you've figured out who I am, I'm sure. The name James was a little misleading. It is my real name, after all. But everyone calls me by my other name now.

Welcome to my story, ladies and gentlemen. I'm Captain Hook.

CHAPTER SEVEN

A few years later

I stood on the deck of the Queen Anne's Revenge, my telescope in hand. It was a quiet night, the ocean water bubbling below. I had become very good at navigating for the crew at night, letting the stars lead the way.

Blackbeard had grown to respect and protect me like a son he had never had. He'd been very impressed with my skills over the years, especially since his right-hand man, Tiny, had perished at the hands of a soulless mermaid. They had the uncanny ability to hypnotize and seduce weak men, and unfortunately, Tiny had succumbed.

You're probably thinking that we abandoned our plan to defeat Pan, choosing a life of pirates instead. It had been a long time to us, but our mission wasn't forgotten.

You see, while it had been three years to us, time ran a little differently in Neverland. Instead of it being a few years, Pan had been trapped for only a few weeks in his eyes. Time ran much slower there.

We had to make sure everything was perfect, a waiting game of sorts. I had told Smee that he was free to go. "You don't have to make this your life."

But Smee just shook his head, a smile playing on his lips. "This is my life now, Hook. This is my choice. I won't leave your side, even after we defeat Pan."

I had been surprised, to say the least. Even Hanzel chose to stay, becoming like an uncle to us. He was very protective and a hard worker on the ship. Blackbeard had grown to appreciate us all.

For some reason, Blackbeard reminded me of Father. They had the same dark eyes and a sense of authority. I had grown to respect and love him just as he had for me. We were all like family to each other. A strange family, but a family nonetheless. It was our form of normal in the chaotic lives we had gotten ourselves into.

Of course, we had to tell Blackbeard about Pan. He was a no-nonsense man so we decided to leave out all of the magic and fairy dust aspects, choosing to tell him about a land full of treasure instead.

"There's an abundance of treasure on Neverland, Captain. Enough to last an entire lifetime I'm sure," I had begun the conversation. "And if you help us find it, it's all yours for the taking. We don't want any of it. That isn't our goal."

"Our plan is to defeat Pan, and we'll need your help," Hanzel commented. He had explained that Pan was very powerful and we couldn't do it alone. "If you help us defeat him, the treasure is yours."

Blackbeard had stroked his thick beard, lost in thought. "And what about ye lost boys?" he had asked.

"We're taking them with us," Smee jumped in. Over the years, he had grown strong and brave, the scared little Smee I remembered long gone. "We have to save them, too."

So, Blackbeard had agreed, our plan coming together better than we could have guessed. We had a crew, money, weapons, and had gained many skills since that night in Neverland.

I smiled as I closed my telescope, confirming we were on the right path. We were on our way to a new uncharted island; an island Blackbeard had heard about during our last quest for treasure. We all had a rough idea of where it was at, but it had taken a few days to find the right way. I had thought we were on the right path, but we had to turn around at one point when the compass switched from East to West.

Over the last few hours, a thick fog had coated the surface of the water below, making it impossible to see very far in front of the ship. I could still see the stars above, but the ocean was a little tricky.

Suddenly, the hairs on my arm prickled like there was electricity in the air. Something was wrong, but what was it? I pulled my telescope out once again. Maybe it was the mermaids, back to steal more of our crew.

"What are ye looking at, Hook?" came Blackbeard's voice. He wasn't usually out at night but would occasionally come out to check on me.

"I'm not sure," I said. "Something doesn't feel right." Blackbeard's back stiffened, alert by my answer. That's one thing that Blackbeard had taught me. Always trust your instincts. Without them, you didn't stand a chance.

I scanned the water ahead, my eyes struggling to find something in the fog. But I couldn't see anything.

"Over here, boy."

I turned, quietly making my way to the other side of the deck where Blackbeard had wandered. Just as I made it to the railing, I saw what he was talking about.

"A ship," I whispered. What was a ship doing all the way out here? "Do you think they heard about the treasure as well?"

"No," came Blackbeard's sharp reply. "It's here for something else. Can you see anything with yer telescope?"

I put the telescope to my left eye, quickly finding the mysterious ship. "There are people on board," I murmured. I couldn't quite see them but as they got closer, I could make out a few figures.

There were a few small men on the deck, pointing in our direction. Something was very familiar about them, but we were in a different time so that couldn't be possible. They looked as though from my own time. Victorian England, I was told it was called. But if we had jumped in time, how could... If we could just get a little closer...

I aimed the telescope at the stern, hoping to find more people aboard. And as I caught sight of someone else, my heart dropped.

A wicked smile engulfed the telescope's lens.

"No," I whispered. "It can't be." Dropping the telescope, I stepped back from the edge of the ship.

"Hook?" came Blackbeard's voice. But I couldn't utter a word.

"Speak, boy. Ye have to tell me. What did ye see?" Blackbeard placed his strong hand on my shoulder, urging me to find my voice.

"It's Pan. He's found us." *And he brought a lot of friends from the looks of it*, I thought.

But Blackbeard didn't hesitate. He was quick to action, like always. I had learned a lot from him while aboard this ship, but I could never be as powerful as a captain. Well, not yet at least.

"Bring a spring upon her cable!" he screamed. This was a command for whoever was at the wheel to come around in a different path. He was planning a surprise maneuver. "Give chase."

We were going right for Pan's ship.

"Hook, find Smee and Hanzel! Get out of here, boy." I nodded, heading straight below deck.

He turned back to his crew, who had all gathered on the deck behind us. "Tonight, we blow the man down." Blackbeard smiled, his gold tooth shining in the dark night.

"Smee! Hanzel!" I screamed, adrenaline filling my veins with each step I took. My pocket began to vibrate, a small glow emitting from the watch.

Pan must be getting close, I thought. "Gather your things, we're leaving! Pan and his crew found us."

Smee jumped from his bunk, bag already packed. He packed it every night before bed. We all knew this day was coming. It had only been a matter of time. It just so happened that time was now.

"What do I tell, ye boys?" we heard Blackbeard scream from above. "Dead men tell no tales!" The rest of the crew recited back, ready for a fight. He was telling them to leave no survivors, although I wasn't so sure it would be that easy.

"Okay, we're ready," Hanzel announced. They had gathered all of their things anticipating the next jump.

"I wonder where we'll go this time," Smee mused. He liked to tell tales of faraway places to all the crew members, hoping one day we would end up there.

I grabbed the watch from my pocket, now glowing bright like a flame.

Click. Click. Click.

But nothing happened. "Not again," Smee said, groaning.

"What do you mean not again?" Hanzel questioned. "This has happened before?"

"It must only work when Pan is right next to us," I concluded. It was the only thing that made sense. When we had tried it on the beach before Pan had reached us, it didn't work. It finally worked when he was within a few feet of the watch.

"Prepare for battle, men! A barrel o'whiskey soon be yers if ye bring me the head of Pan!" Blackbeard's voice washed over me like a bucket of cold water.

"We'll have to fight," I realized. It wasn't the worst thing in the world, but I had to admit I was very afraid. It would be my first battle after all. Luckily, we had been training every day with the crew; Blackbeard had been kind enough to give us all swords. I also had my hook, of course, so in many ways I was well equipped.

Smee's smile lit the dark and dingy quarters, his new bravery engulfing his face. "Dead men tell no tales, they say." He winked.

"Aye, aye," Hanzel agreed. "We knew this day would come, Hook. We're ready for whatever happens." They both pulled their swords from their scabbards, a new addition to our wardrobe. Blackbeard had given them to us the same night we got our swords.

"Best way to carry it," he had explained.

Weapons in hand we made our way up to the deck, ready for whatever came our way.

"What are ye boys doing?" Blackbeard's voice boomed. His eyes flashed with surprise, expecting us to be far away by now.

"We're here to fight." Hanzel smiled.

"And fight we shall!" Smee yelled. I nodded at our Captain, showing him that everything was okay. We were about to fight the most powerful person I knew, and I didn't want to distract him.

Blackbeard took a deep breath, coming to terms with the new plan. "All right, ye foolish men." He winked. "Try and keep up."

Just then I caught sight of Pan's full ship. Nibs and the twins had swords of their own, looks of pure hatred covering their face. So, they had believed Pan's story.

I scanned the rest of the deck, noticing plenty of fairies and the rest of the lost boys. It looked as though he had recruited more, but many of them seemed much older. *Was he really that desperate?* I asked myself.

Also, on board were many creatures from Neverland, including a one-eyed man creature they called Smorf, a few goblins that lived deep in the forest, and a girl I had never seen before. She had bright red hair and seemed to be glowing.

"When I yell boom about, ye scoundrels hit the deck," whispered Blackbeard.

Pan's ship was fast approaching, our battle seconds away. He stared right at me, a smug smile coating his lips. He looked as though the battle had already been won. Little did he know, a war had just begun.

Our crew had been armed to the teeth. Every man carried a sword. Many also carried a Blunderbuss on their other side. The gun, while not the most effective, came in handy on many of our journeys over the last few years.

Mullins and Turk, two of our men, armed the cannons. "Fire in the hole!" they screamed as Pan's ship lined up with ours. A large blast echoed in the night air. Sparks flew as a cannon barreled right through one of Pan's sails.

I heard a loud crash as a makeshift bridge slammed down on our deck, the twins and a few of the new lost boys sprinting across with their weapons in hand seconds later. The older boys soon took aim at Blackbeard, whose laughter echoed loudly as, one by one, they failed.

Smee and Hanzel were taking on two of the goblins, their swords ricocheting right off their hard skin. Goblins were notoriously hard to fight, the only way to kill them being a bullet right through the heart. I remembered this from all the days working on the boat with Pan and how he would talk about Neverland and its beings. They didn't know that, however.

"Mullins, your gun!" I yelled. Mullins quickly turned to me, throwing his gun right into my hand with expert precision. "Smee, Hanzel, you have to shoot them through the heart!" I desperately tossed the gun as Hanzel rolled away from the goblin, his right hand catching the gun right before it hit the ground.

Bang! The tallest goblin hit the deck, a force powerful enough to send Smee to the ground as well.

"Smee!" I screamed, terrified my closest friend was about to be ripped apart. Goblins tore your flesh right off, leaving no chance of survival.

Bang! Another shot rang out, the other goblin falling just as fast as the first. Smee scurried away in search of his sword, which laid right under the ship's wheel.

"Traitor!" I turned just as the twins made their way for me.

"You don't understand!" I screamed. "Pan isn't what you think! I didn't steal the magic. You have to get as far away from him as you can." I didn't want to hurt the twins. They were the most naïve of all the lost boys. They didn't know any better.

"We'll kill you!" they both screamed. "You were nothing to us then, and you are nothing to us now!" Their small eyes turned menacing as they gripped their swords and circled me.

"Boom about!" Blackbeard shouted above the noise of all the chaos. I quickly dropped to my knees, not knowing what was about to happen. Just then, the giant wooden boom came barreling across the deck. The twins' eyes locked in horror as they were smacked across the deck and over the rail of the ship.

Splash.

I didn't even have time to register what had happened before I heard another voice taunting me. "I told you I'd find you, Ace. Now give me my watch." His vicious face followed my every move as I stood back up, sword in hand.

"Never," I vowed. "And my name isn't Ace. It's Hook. Ace is long gone, Pan." I shifted into a fighting stance, one leg in front of the other.

Pan smiled, encouraging the challenge. He loved to fight; it was the only time he could let the violence trapped inside out.

"Well, what are you waiting for, Hook?" he mocked. "Don't you want to kill me? Just like you tried to kill Neverland." There was a twinkle in his eye. He knew he was lying, but the others believed him without a doubt.

"I did no such thing!" I yelled, anger overtaking my body. I launched myself at him, my sword smashing full force into his. He took a step back, throwing his sword from side to side, a maneuver meant to distract me.

I dropped to my knees, swinging my sword low. I was hoping to sweep him right off his feet, a move that had worked in the past when practicing. I wasn't so lucky, however.

Pan jumped high, hovering above the ground. "Well, look what we have here. It looks like you've learned some new moves." Pan laughed. He swung his sword down with both hands, a shot meant to kill.

I rolled to the side as quick as I could, but I wasn't quite fast enough. The sharp edge of the blade sliced down my back, leaving a fiery trail in its path.

I groaned in pain. This wasn't going how I had hoped. We came this far for nothing; I was about to lose the battle once and for all. For nothing.

"Hook!" Blackbeard cried in horror. I looked behind Pan. Blackbeard's tall frame practically engulfed Pan's. He swung his sword, aiming straight for Pan's heart. Pan quickly moved out of the way, momentarily distracted by his new enemy.

I struggled to my feet, searching the deck for the sword I had dropped during our skirmish. The sound of metal crashing against metal was all I could hear, a skilled duel playing out between Blackbeard and Pan.

If I could just find the stupid sword, I thought.

"Arg!" someone sputtered, falling to the ground wounded. I quickly looked up, expecting one of the older lost boys or maybe even Pan to be flailing on the deck in pain.

But it was Blackbeard. "No!" I screamed, louder than I had ever screamed before. This couldn't be happening.

Blackbeard gripped the middle of his body, his face a mask of pure pain. I looked over at Pan, who stood a few feet away. His shirt was torn and a trail of blood oozed down his arm. So, he had been injured.

I reached into my pocket, pulling the glowing watch out for Pan to see. "Is this what you want?" I screamed. I had to get him away from Blackbeard. Another person couldn't die because of me.

I threw the watch across the small stretch of ocean, landing in a pile of rope on the bow of Pan's ship.

"Just like that," Pan said weakly, blood loss obviously taking its toll on him. "I always knew you were a coward, Ace."

I bristled at the use of his nickname for me, the urge to fight quickly returning.

"Come on, boys! We have what we came for," Pan said. They all quickly exited the ship, returning to their own. Setting sail, they were lost in the fog just as quick as they had arrived.

I stumbled over to Blackbeard, my wound momentarily forgotten.

"The watch," he whispered, unable to speak much more. "Why?"

"It was just a fake," I explained. "He'll figure it out soon enough, but for the time being, we should be fine." I ripped off my sash and applied it to his wound. Blood quickly soaked it through. A dreadful feeling entered my gut.

"It's too late, Hook. Ye captain is not going to make it," he said sadly. There were no tears in his eyes, but I knew this moment was just as heartbreaking for him as it was for me.

Smee and Hanzel were quick to my side, taking Blackbeard into his private quarters to say his final words to me.

"I've loved ye like a son, boy." Blackbeard took a big, shaky breath. "It's only right that you take over as captain of the ship."

I shook my head, the thought never occurring to me. "You're going to be okay, sir. You're the captain of this ship, not me. I could never do something like that."

"Ye are destined for it, Hook. I know ye don't see it now, but ye will one day." His eyes fluttered, the energy draining from his body as fast as the blood. "Just promise me you will defeat Pan." I nodded, unable to speak. I had no words for a moment like this. My heart was breaking. Anger simmered just below the surface. "I want to have died for something," he stated.

"I promise," I choked out, grabbing his hand.

Blackbeard smiled, a new look forming. His breathing became shallow as the seconds ticked by until, finally, it ceased.

"I promise," I repeated. "Pan will die, if it's the last thing I do."

Minutes later, I emerged from the private quarters to the crew standing silently, an expectant look on their faces.

"Captain Blackbeard is gone," I announced. Smee and Hanzel bowed their heads. They would see this loss just as I have, a fuel to our already raging fire.

The rest of the crew stood somberly. A crew without a Captain is no crew at all. I saw it on all their faces.

"You will lead us then," Mullins announced. I glanced in his direction, surprise covering my face. Why would they want me as their captain? Surely, he was mistaken.

"Aye, aye!" they all screamed in unison.

"I agree," Smee proclaimed. There was a look of determination on his face. Had Blackbeard talked to him about this before?

"Aye." Hanzel winked.

They all seemed to think I was the logical choice to lead them, as confusing as it seemed. Filled with a newfound sense of responsibility, Blackbeard's words echoing in my head, I rose to the challenge.

"All right, ye scoundrels," I joked. A fond memory we would have of our fallen captain. The crew laughed, despite the heaviness of the situation.

"So, what's the plan?" Smee asked. "Since you're captain and all."

I smiled, the title growing on me faster than I would have thought.

"We stay the course," I announced. "Find the island and capture the treasure."

***

Later that night, we had sent Blackbeard on his final voyage, laying him to rest in the ocean below, something he had always demanded when it was his time to go. We all watched as he drifted away, the ocean swallowing him whole, a true testament to the life he had chosen.

"Never forgotten, never replaced, forever in our thoughts, his memory never displaced," we had chanted.

It was early afternoon now, and the sun beat down on us all. According to the map, we would see the island any minute. I readied my things, my mind lost in thought.

Don't let me die for nothing, Blackbeard's voice echoed in my head.

I won't. I promise, I kept repeating.

I tucked my sword into my new sash, something Hanzel had handed me the night before. My bag full of survival tools, and a canteen full of water, I headed back to the deck.

"We'll be dropping anchor any second, Captain," came Turk's voice. He was a giant of a man with a thick curly mustache and big, round belly.

"Aye, Turk." I turned to Smee, commanding him to get the dinghy ready for our departure. Smee, Hanzel, and a few of the other crew members had volunteered to come ashore with me for this leg of the journey. The rest of the crew had to stay behind to protect the ship from any other pirates.

We were in the middle of nowhere, but when it came to our lifestyle, it was better to be safe than sorry.

"Is everyone ready?" I asked.

"Aye, Captain. We have plenty of water and supplies to get us through for a few days. We shouldn't be gone that long, but we have the room so I figured it wouldn't hurt." Hanzel motioned to the back of the dinghy, which was as full as he could probably get it.

"How are you feeling?" he whispered.

"I'm okay," I assured him. "It isn't what I expected, but in order to defeat Pan, it's the best chance we've got."

He nodded, agreeing with me for the time being. "Absolutely," he said. "Whatever it takes." His eyes flashed again, thinking of Pan. He had more reasons to hate him now, but he always managed to stay focused. I was very impressed with that.

We all climbed aboard the small ship, watching it lower closer and closer toward the calm ocean as Mullins pulled the lever that dropped us down.

I pulled the treasure map from my pocket, glancing it over once more. "Once we get to the shore, it says we head straight for the woods," I confirmed out loud.

Hanzel turned to me, hands busy sharpening his sword on a stone he had gotten on our last adventure. "And then what?" he asked.

"And then we search for the temple said to hold this buried treasure," I confirmed. According to the map, it was just a few hundred paces into the trees. *It won't be too hard to find*, I thought.

As we pulled the dinghy ashore, Smee grabbed the attached rope and tied it to a large tree trunk. We all gathered our things, making sure our weapons were secure and supplies intact.

"Well, then, men." I didn't know what to say. This was my first mission as Captain after all, once again thrown out of my comfort zone. "To the temple, we go."

CHAPTER EIGHT

As we made our way through the forest, the trees and bushes flush with life, I began to ponder what our next move would be after we secured the treasure. I knew it was there. Blackbeard was never wrong when it came to things like this.

And if that wasn't enough, my instincts told me this was an important place. Blackbeard must have felt it, too. Somehow, finding this treasure was a piece of the puzzle to defeating Pan. I knew it in my heart.

Glancing at the map one more time, I noticed we were only a few paces away from the mysterious temple. While I had never seen something like it before, I was certain it would stick out like a sore thumb in a jungle like this.

"We're almost there," I announced. "It should be just behind this thicket of trees."

We all grabbed our swords, slashing through the dense plants to clear a path until we reached the other side. Leaves and branches fell all around us, insects scurrying away at the disturbance.

I was the first to step out, the forest now lost behind us. The ground was as flat as the deck of our ship, bright grass kissing our boots. Smee and Hanzel quickly followed suit, the rest of the small crew right behind them.

"Well isn't that something," Smee whispered in awe. He looked straight ahead, eyes round and full of disbelief.

"I've never seen anything like it," Hanzel agreed. He had one hand on his forehead to shield his eyes from the bright sun above, his neck stretched up to take in the giant structure in front of us.

The temple stood as tall as the surrounding trees, solid stone sinking into the flat ground below. Skinny vines wrapped around each level with beautiful flowers sprouting out in every color imaginable. What looked to be about a hundred steps led up to what I assumed was the entrance.

"I guess that's where we need to go," came Smee's voice, a hint of amusement laced within. He always loved adventures, and this was proving to be a very interesting one so far.

As we made our way up, step by step, I pulled the map out once again. We had made it to the temple, but the trail continued once we got inside. Our journey wasn't ending anytime soon, by the looks of it.

"What happens when we get inside?" asked the furthest man back. We called him Stinky, but you probably don't want to know why. He was a stocky fellow but hard-hitting, his thick blonde beard gleaming in the daylight.

"I'm not sure," came my hesitant reply. The map got very complicated once we entered the temple, the path weaving and curving in different directions. "We follow this path." I pointed at the map and held it up. "And the treasure should be at the end of the trail."

Stinky grunted in agreement. He wasn't a man of many words, but he was one of the strongest in the crew. That was why I asked him to come along. He always came in handy in places like this.

"I wonder what the treasure is," Smee commented.

"It's probably just more gold," Hanzel decided. I knew he was distracted by the thought of Pan, his sister's revenge on his mind. Not to mention the loss of Blackbeard. I didn't think it was possible to have more hatred for Pan, but we had all been proven wrong.

I shook my head, my gut telling me something different. "Remember when Blackbeard told us to always trust our instincts?" I asked. They nodded in agreement. "Well, my instincts tell me that whatever is inside will help us defeat Pan."

Hanzel blinked, a small smile appeared, his distraction momentarily gone. "It always works out, doesn't it?" he mused.

"Well, what are we waiting for then?" Smee smiled in excitement, now standing at the edge of the entrance.

Laughing at his enthusiasm, I took a big step forward, making my way into the temple. There was a second of complete darkness before a small bright light appeared in the corner of my eye.

"To protect the souls on which he preys, the secret to Pan lies at the end of this maze," came a mysterious voice. There wasn't a soul in sight, the voice radiating from the temple itself.

"Where did that come from?" Smee whispered. He was standing right next to me, his sword gripped firmly in his hand.

"I don't know," I replied. The bright light suddenly grew larger and I soon realized that what looked to be a small log had caught fire. *How did that happen?* I thought.

"I think we're supposed to use it to light the way," Hanzel said. "We'll need it to see the treasure map." He calmly walked over to the torch and picked it up, revealing the entrance of the maze the ominous voice had explained.

"It looks like it goes all the way down to the bottom of the temple," I noticed, glancing at the map. "That would explain all of the twists and turns."

"Let's get this over with," Stinky muttered, obviously upset that it would take so long. "We haven't got all day." Although he was the perfect man for adventures such as this, he had a real distaste for walking long distances.

Grabbing our items, we continued on the path, carefully following every curve of the map. At one point, however, we took a wrong turn and nearly fell to our deaths. There didn't seem to be any protection from the edge, the dusty path merely dropping right off into oblivion.

Keeping that in mind, we continued on our way, taking every turn as careful as we could. We were nearing the end now, the treasure said to be just a few turns away. I readied myself, not knowing what to expect.

"Grab your weapons, everyone," I said. "Be ready for anything. We don't know what could be at the end of this maze." Though my instincts told me it was important, it was better to be safe than sorry.

I tucked the map back into my pocket and grabbed the sword from my sash. I had grown very comfortable with my hook now, which doubled as an extra weapon.

As we rounded the final corner, a large room appeared before us. The same skinny vines with beautiful flowers that covered the outside of the temple now clung to the walls of its bottom floor. Only this time they were glowing, illuminating the room in soft colors.

Sitting atop a large boulder directly in the middle of the room was a small Native American woman with long black hair, a red and white feather peeking out from behind her head. Her eyes were closed.

"I knew you would be coming, Hook," she said, pleased. Her eyes popped open, an encouraging smile appearing on her delicate face. Her light voice echoed in the spacious room, the flowers growing bright with excitement at the sound.

"Who are you? And how do you know who I'm?" I asked the mysterious woman. My crew had surrounded me in response to this new situation, standing armed by my side just in case.

"My name is Tiger Lily," she said simply. "And you are here to defeat Pan."

Had Blackbeard sent word that we were coming? How could she possibly know who I was or what I wanted? I knew by now that not everything could be explained, but that didn't stop me from trying to figure it out.

"I have much to tell you about Pan, but first I must give you this." She held her small hands out, a clock resting upon them. It was square and black, the hands ticking as each second went by. Flecks of gold covered the surface, standing out against the rest of its frame. "It's a clock much like the watch you have. It'll take you to where you need to go next."

I stepped forward, accepting her gift. "Thank you," I said. "But how will I know when to use it?" Pan's watch only activated when he was near. This one seemed to be a little different.

"It knows where you need to go and when the time will be. Don't worry about that," she assured me, leaving me just as confused.

Stepping down from the boulder, she came around until we were face to face. "You have more to learn, dear boy. Come, let us sit down so I can ease your mind." Her gentle hands motioned ahead for me to follow. Confused as to how all of this was happening, and curious about the opportunity of having all my questions answered, I signaled Smee and the rest of the crew to follow close behind.

We were soon seated atop smaller boulders, our feet resting on the floor. While it wasn't the most comfortable seat in the world, I didn't mind. And neither did the others. It had been a long walk, and it was nice to rest our feet.

"Pan is more powerful than you have imagined," Tiger Lily began. She had lit a small fire. our seats forming an O around its edges.

"He has been controlling your dreams and manipulating your reality," she explained. "That night he found you on Hanzel's floor, he had entered your nightmare, making you think he was near. That's how he found where you were."

"But how could he do that?" I asked. It wasn't possible to enter someone's dreams like that, was it?

"It's a part of his power. He does it with fairy dust. Not quite as powerful as Starstuff but still capable of being used in dangerous ways." Tiger Lily threw another piece of wood onto the flame, causing it to swirl higher. "That's what he used to find your ship as well," she continued. "When your compass failed, switching directions suddenly, it was just a trick." Her explanation sent a shiver up my spine. "It was a mirage meant to steer you toward Neverland."

Tiger Lily's eyes grew dark and serious. She wrung her hands together in deep thought. "He will do whatever it takes to get his watch back. Including killing you," she concluded.

That I had already known, but it still made me feel uneasy when hearing it out loud. I was afraid I didn't stand a chance at defeating someone who could enter my dreams or play with my mind like Pan could.

"So, what do we do?" Hanzel asked. He rested his chin on top of his hand, his face a mix of concern and bewilderment.

"You have to kill him. It's the only way to save Neverland and everyone on it," she said simply. A small smile began to curve her lips, her eyes moving directly to mine. "And it's foretold that you are the only one who can do it, Hook."

My eyebrows raised in surprise. "And how am I supposed to do that?"

Tiger Lily laughed, shaking her head at my reaction. "Well, that's the ultimate question, isn't it? You see, the answer to that can be found on a small island called Barrie. On the island, you will find a cave, a few hundred paces up the hill. Inside the cave is the secret to defeating Pan."

The flames danced all around, small sparks spitting at the edge.

My head spun with so many questions. How did we find Barrie? Why was I the one foretold to kill Pan? How did the watch know when to jump? And how did I know if I could trust this person?

But before I could ask any of them, the fire roared to life, doubling in both height and heat. Smee and Hanzel both jumped to my side, one hand resting on each of my shoulders. The clock, which I held in the palm of my hand, began to glow bright like the flames.

"I think it's happening!" I yelled, answering my final question. As the light grew brighter and brighter, Hanzel and Smee remained stuck to my sides.

Suddenly, we were sucked into the light, our bodies pulled through galaxies and stars once again. I noticed that this time it had only taken Hanzel and Smee with me, leaving everyone else behind. *It must be because-*

But before I could even finish the thought, we were spat out onto another pile of sand. I opened my eyes, closing them just as quick at the sun's blinding light.

"Where is everyone else?" came Smee's voice. I opened my eyes once again, letting them finally adjust to wherever we were.

Smee was dusting off the dark brown smattering all over his hat. I quickly realized it wasn't sand that we had landed on. It was dirt. And there was a lot of it.

As I looked up, I noticed large, dried pieces of plant life that tumbled across the dirty ground. It was completely flat for as far as I could see. I turned around, hoping I could find some type of clue as to where we were. But instead, I was confronted with a larger group of men, their hands armed with some type of gun.

The man standing in front had a shiny medallion attached to his chest and very pointy shoes.

"I'm the sheriff in these here parts," came his gravelly voice. "Now what are you men doing here?" His lower lip looked swollen with something as he spat on the ground.

I paused, considering what to say to these strange men. They all had a face full of stubble, their dusty clothes worn and well used as more of those strange, dried plants tumbled behind them.

"We were just passing through," came Hanzel's confident voice. He had met a lot of people over the years and dealt with them very well. "We don't mean to bother you, sheriff."

What in the world is a sheriff? I thought.

The men all took a big step forward, their guns shining as the sun beat down on us all. I had never seen a gun like theirs before. It was smaller than the Blunderbusses I was now used to, but somehow looked even more powerful.

"What kind of a gun is that?" I wondered aloud.

The sheriff's eyes turned to me, glancing at the hook on my right hand. His eyes narrowed in concern, questioning the real reason as to why we were here. We obviously didn't belong, our flowy shirts a complete contrast to their dusty clothes.

"Colt 45," he said simply, spitting something onto the ground once again. "The best gun in the west." He signaled to his men, a subtle head nod in our direction. Confused, I looked at Hanzel. Perhaps he knew what was going on.

"Just do what they say," Hanzel whispered lowly, so the men couldn't hear. Smee and I nodded, taking our friend's word. There was no doubt in our minds that Hanzel knew what was best in a situation like this.

"It seems we have a problem here, boys." The sheriff's lips turned up in a smile. It wasn't an evil look but it was far from a friendly one. "People don't just pass through these parts unless they're robbers or wanted men."

His dusty sidekicks had arrived at our sides, pulling us up from the ground. I wiped the back of my clothes, removing all the dirt I could with one hand.

"Well, I can assure you, sheriff, that we're just passing through." I smiled, hoping he would believe me. It wasn't like I was lying, really. This wasn't our final stop; I was sure of that. We had to find Barrie, and judging by the looks of this place, it wasn't anywhere near here.

"You caught me on a good day, I suppose," the sheriff said. As those words left his mouth, a strange feeling entered my gut.

He wasn't going to let us go. But what was he going to do with us?

"I'm glad to hear that," came Hanzel's confident voice once again. "We'll just be on our way, if you could—" His words quickly got cut off.

"It's not going to be that easy, you see." The sheriff's smile returned, his comrades following suit. They pulled out what seemed to be three pairs of handcuffs, different from the ones I had known in England.

"But we didn't do anything wrong," Smee's quiet voice said in disbelief. He knew just as well as I did that no matter what we said to these men they were going to do as they pleased. But he couldn't help it, his fists balling in frustration.

"Now how do I know that?" the sheriff taunted. "I wouldn't be doing my job if I didn't bring you in, now would I?" He winked at Smee, his face smug and proud. He liked locking people up, took pride in apprehending wanderers like us.

His men forced our hands behind our backs, quickly fastening the locks until the cuffs held tight. I didn't bother to struggle, instead trusting Hanzel and his word to do what they said.

Besides, if we were really in danger, the clock Tiger Lily had given us would have sucked us back in again. My instincts knew that much at least.

"Walk," came one of the men's deep voices, pushing me into action. Smee and Hanzel joined my side, one of the other men joining us together with some form of rope. He tied it around our middle, looping it from me to Smee and then Smee to Hanzel.

The sheriff grabbed the slack, jumping onto a massive black horse. It neighed in response, adjusting to the weight of his load. He quickly tied the end of the rope to the saddle's horn, assuring we wouldn't run off from wherever we were headed.

The other men quickly jumped onto their horses as well, beginning a slow trot in the direction of the sun. It was beginning to set. A beautiful array of pinks and oranges colored the sky.

"Where are we going?" I asked.

"Like I said before," came the sheriff's gravelly voice, "we're taking you in. But we have a stop to make first."

I looked at Hanzel, a question in my eyes. What could he possibly have to stop for before taking us to his town?

Hanzel raised his shoulders, no idea as to what was going to happen next. We still had our supplies, the shortest man jimmying it to the pack on the back of his saddle. We would have to find a way to escape. But we had been in far worse situations before, so I wasn't going to let myself worry about it too much. There was always a way.

***

By the time the sun had almost completely disappeared, we had figured out the sheriff's quest. He had captured a man by the name of Hopalong. He was a rough looking man with a wooden leg, causing him to hop with each step. He had a handkerchief tied around his neck and a leather vest covering his dusty shirt.

"You know what I want," the sheriff told him. "Just tell me where your brother is and I'll let you go. That's all there is to it."

But Hopalong just smiled, disgust lacing his voice as he replied, "You know I'll never do that. You might as well kill me now, sheriff. I'll never help you."

The sheriff just shook his head, disappointment clear on his face. Whoever Hopalong's brother was, the sheriff seemed to want him very badly. His frustration was now replaced by cockiness.

"Have it your way then," he grumbled, adding Hopalong to our loop of ropes.

We all began walking again, heading for whatever town they called home.

"Who are you?" Hopalong asked. He was looking at Hanzel, the closest man to him. He kept up surprisingly well with that leg of his, his hop barely slowing him down. He must have had it for a long time.

"The name's Hanzel. This is Smee and Hook." He gestured to us both. We nodded our heads in greeting, keeping pace with the trotting horses.

"You don't look like you're from around here," he said, smiling. "And what happened to your hand? Is that why they call you Hook?"

Despite the situation, I laughed. "Yes, that's why they call me Hook. It happened… in a fight," I finished. "This was the only thing we could find, but it seems to be working for the time being."

Hopalong nodded his head in agreement. "Don't I know that," he exclaimed, smacking his wooden leg on the ground. "Got my leg trapped in the railway when I fell off my horse a few years back. Luckily, my brother was there to save me. He knew a doctor, got me fixed up right away. And I've been walking with a hop in my step ever since!"

"Quiet!" the sheriff yelled. "No more talking until we get to the station."

Hopalong rolled his eyes in a moment of defiance but shut his mouth.

The town was small and dirty. The road consisted of solidly packed dirt covered in horse shit and other muck. The buildings lined up in a neat row, side by side. We marched down what was obviously the main street. All were made of wood and

110

looked worn by time, built in a place that was clearly didn't welcome them any more than it welcomed us.

A few minutes later, we reached our destination. A small building made of brick – the only building in town made of brick actually – stood at the edge of the town. It had a wooden deck attached to its front, the word *JAIL* scrawled across the top in messy black lettering.

The sheriff's men quickly dismounted their large horses, tying them to the rail attached to the deck.

"Welcome to jail, boys." The sheriff's cocky attitude returned as he motioned for his men to bring us inside. "I do hope you enjoy your stay." He winked.

Two of his men led us inside, pulling the rope at one end like we were horses. We came around a corner to two rooms with iron bars taking up a vast majority of the space.

"Home, sweet home," one of the men said. He ushered us all into one cell, taking the rope with him as he exited. We still had our arms bound by cuffs, but moving around became much easier once there was no rope.

"Sweet dreams," another one said, smirking. And just like that, they exited the jail. Going home for the night, I assumed. No doubt they would see us come morning.

"Don't worry. It really isn't that bad. You won't be in here for long. The sheriff just likes to play games with new faces he meets. His way of *keeping the peace,* as he calls it." Hopalong snorted, shaking his head in disgust. "If you ask me, I think he just likes the power. Likes to remind people he's in charge."

In a way, the sheriff reminded me of Pan. Using his power for evil instead of good. There would always be bad people in the world, no matter the location, unfortunately. That was a lesson I had learned early on as a pirate. We had met a lot of fellows like that.

Hopalong made himself comfortable, obviously a frequent guest of the jail cell we were currently in.

"Do you come here often?" I asked after a while, keeping my voice light.

I was genuinely curious because I liked Hopalong. His wooden leg reminded me very much of my own makeshift hook hand. We had something in common. Besides, we were all getting bored just sitting there looking and smelling each other. The walk had been long and now the cell was full of the lingering body odor of four grown men.

"Oh yes," he agreed. "He's been after my brother for a long time and seems to think the only way to catch him is through me."

112

"Why is that?" Smee asked. He was sitting on the ground right in front of Hopalong, his legs crossed at the ankles.

Hopalong shrugged. "My brother is in the business of getting what he wants." He smirked. "And what he wants usually involves stealing a lot of money."

We all laughed in unison. "Well, that's something we can relate to, isn't it?" Hanzel said, slapping his knee.

"That it's," I agreed. I took a seat next to Smee, all of us seated on the cold floor of the cell now.

"So, where are you men from?" Hopalong asked. "I know you aren't from around here with clothes like that."

I looked at Hanzel once again. While I had grown to like Hopalong, I knew we couldn't tell him where we were from. Magic wasn't something he would believe in, his world a far stretch from the land we were used to.

"We come from far away," Hanzel said simply, shrugging his shoulders. "That's all we can really tell you. This is just a stop along the way, a detour of sorts."

Hopalong nodded, accepting our answer for what it was. He knew what it was like to keep secrets I had guessed, so he knew not to press for more.

"Well, I think I can help with that." He smiled, sitting up. We had been in the cell for a couple of hours, the small window now void of any light as the sun disappeared until morning.

"What do you mean?" Smee asked. "How can—"

A loud crash echoed through the jail. Smee and Hanzel both covered their heads as debris fell above us. Dust filled my lungs, forcing me to cough violently.

"Look alive, brother," came a strong voice. I quickly wiped my eyes, trying to see what had happened. "We haven't got all night."

Hopalong pulled me to my feet, his face lit with the biggest smile I had ever seen. "Time to go," he stated.

Still dazed and confused, I jumped into action. The blast had broken through the back wall of the cell, breaking the iron bars in front. I quickly stepped around the debris to the front of the station where the sheriff's men had stashed our belongings.

Hanzel came running behind me to help grab our things. "I didn't expect that," he yelled, his ears still adjusting to the blast.

"Come on!" Smee yelled. He was standing near the broken wall, the dark sky filled with stars behind him. Hopalong was busy mounting a horse, a tall man directly to his left.

I eagerly glanced around, looking for the telltale green sign of our bag.

"There!" Hanzel pointed his finger at the chair behind the desk. The bag was hanging from the side, as if the blast had never happened. I quickly grabbed our things, and Hanzel and I met them all outside. My heart raced at lightning speed. I was sure the sheriff and his men were mere seconds away.

"I told you I could help," Hopalong announced proudly. He had finally mounted his horse, his wooden leg stuck awkwardly out from the side. "Quickly, grab a horse and let's get going!"

It was then that I noticed the other men. The man I assumed to be Hopalong's brother sat tall on his horse, his face a stone mask. I couldn't tell if he was happy or mad, but he didn't seem to mind that Hopalong was inviting us to go.

There were several others seated upon getaway animals of their own, their faces covered with different colors of handkerchiefs. Three smaller geldings stood at their side, the saddles empty.

Smee quickly mounted the closest horse, a brown and white beauty with a long flowing mane. Hanzel followed suit, taking his place on a chestnut one with a dark bushy tail. I was the last to climb on, my horse a mixture of white and tan, her blue eyes shining in the dark.

I still was unsure what was happening, but I didn't stop to question it. Getting out of jail was one of my top priorities at the moment so I was happy to go along. Plus, I had to admit it gave me a little bit of joy thinking about the sheriff's face when he came so see us.

"It's nice to meet you fellas," Hopalong's brother said, shaking my good hand. "Sorry for the mess, but it was the quickest way to get y'all out." He had on a leather vest of his own, only black. His dark blue shirt and red handkerchief matched his brother's, something they had undoubtedly done on purpose.

"I'm Hook, and these are my men." I gestured to Smee and Hanzel. They quickly introduced themselves, shaking everyone's hand as well.

"This is my brother," Hopalong proudly exclaimed, a look of admiration painted on his face.

"The name's Butch Cassidy. Don't forget it," came his brother's voice. He quickly tipped his hat, grabbing the reigns of his saddle. "Now let's get out of here before that idiot sheriff figures out where you are."

His ankles grazed the belly of his horse, a command of action. We all did the same, our horses taking off in a full sprint as we made our getaway. We disappeared into the night, leaving a trail of dust as the town disappeared behind us.

It's time for a new adventure, I thought. And what an adventure it would be.

CHAPTER NINE

I found out what happened back at the temple much later, during a series of events you will find out as you read further into my tale. For now, I can relate to you the account I was told.

Meanwhile, back at the temple...

Tiger Lily and the left behind crew were still surrounding the makeshift fire. My men had sought refuge in the temple after our trio didn't return. The storm kicking up didn't help matters either. They were cold and wet and that makes for cranky pirates.

They had been chatting about their adventures throughout the years, Tiger Lily explaining she had come to the temple with the rest of her people many moons ago. The young ones gathered around close, their faces glowing from the flames while their eyes showed a keen interest the older ones lacked.

"I was very little," she began. "I don't remember much, only that my people needed a safe place to go. We were in a war of some kind, our people greatly outnumbered." Her eyebrows dipped low, sadness creeping in as she reminisced on her life. "Pan had come to us in the middle of the night, claiming he could save us from it all. He promised we would have our own land and could grow whatever we desired. My people immediately believed him, of course. They had no other choice; we were dead without him."

Slowly standing up, she walked to the wall and grabbed one of the glowing flowers. She tucked it behind her ear, grabbing a stick on her way back. As she came back to her seat, she began to draw, using the stick to carve what seemed to be a man and a woman holding hands.

"So, we ended up in Neverland," she continued. "Pan had promised us a blessed place, and as it turned out, he surprised us with a whole temple of our own to call home."

The fire burned bright, spitting and popping as she carried on with her story. "But it was, of course, too good to be true, we soon learned." She had finished her drawing, the man and woman looking remarkably like her. They had the same kind eyes and were adorned with feathers in their hair.

"He began to control my people, giving us all jobs both above and below ground. We soon realized he controlled every aspect of our day."

"For the elders, he would demand to know everything about our wise ways and beautiful traditions. He would argue with them day and night, claiming we all had magic in our blood," she spat out. Her face was now a mixture of disgust and distaste.

"He began calling for volunteers. My family volunteered, hoping he would leave us alone once he discovered he was wrong. There was no magic in our blood, as far as we knew."

Stinky leaned forward unconsciously, the story captivating him like no other.

"So, he drew our blood, drawing the wisdom of our ancestors right out of us and into a small jar." She shook her head, a small laugh escaping. her "We soon found out that he was right. When mixed with fairy dust, our blood became very powerful."

"What happened then?" Starkey asked, his stubbly face glowing in the fire as he, too, became entranced by this short tale.

"He kept taking more of our blood, mixing our wisdom and sacred ways with his precious fairy dust. Once he had enough, he demanded that we create a powerful object with it, capable of transporting him wherever he wanted to go." Her hands gestured above her head, drawing an arc as she went.

"That seemed senseless to us. To transport someone wherever they wanted, at any given moment?" She laughed. The rest of the men joined in, knowing it was possible after all. They had seen it themselves just minutes ago.

"We had no idea at the time. Many of my people told him that such a thing was unheard of. But he persisted, explaining that anything was possible if you tried hard enough." Tiger Lily sighed.

"One day he had gotten angry with some of the elders, claiming they were lying to him on purpose. He said that we had already figured out how to make the clock, using our blood and fairy dust to power it inside. He went on a rampage, cursing our people and destroying our crops. He kept repeating that we were ungrateful for all we were given and deserved to be punished for keeping secrets from him." Tiger Lily's dark brown eyes suddenly filled with tears, her fists clenching at her sides.

"That's when he grabbed my mother and father. To make an example out of them he had said. He took them to the center of our living area, just behind this wall back here." She gestured to the far wall, behind the massive boulder she had been sitting on when we arrived.

"All of my people gathered around, pleading and screaming for Pan to stop. If we could have just a few extra days, we could surely figure it out." It was then that Stinky realized the picture she had drawn on the ground was that of her parents. His gut clenched, a bad feeling eating him from the inside. He may have been a pirate at heart, but he was still human.

"They didn't stand a chance, didn't even see it coming," Tiger Lily began to cry, her quiet sobs breaking the hearts of all the men there. There were a few silent moments, the men anxious for her next words.

After composing herself, she continued. "He didn't listen. Just shook his head and smiled the most vicious grin I have ever seen."

Chills ran up the men's arms, visions of a cruel and evil man dancing throughout their heads.

"His sword pierced their hearts, taking the light from their eyes right in front of me." She paused. "And then he disappeared in a puff of smoke."

The group sat quietly, letting Tiger Lily make peace with her past.

"The elders quickly put a protection spell on the temple, something they had learned when playing with their blood and fairy dust," she said, her foot wiping away her creation in the dirt. "A few hours later someone had a vision of a time traveling object, similar to the one Pan had explained. In her vision, our blood was also mixed with dust from these flowers," she said, pulling the blossom from her hair.

"And that's when we made the clock," she explained. "The rest of the elders sat down that night, the power of their blood stronger than ever. We had finally figured it out." Her small smile momentarily took away the pain on her face. The group sighed in relief.

"It was then foretold, by the gods above, that a mysterious Hook-Man would come to take it away. We didn't know when, of course, but have waited many years for this day to come," she explained. "He is the key to saving our people, saving all of Neverland as well. There is a war raging above, and we're all in grave danger. Throughout the years, we have done whatever we could to keep it safe, many of our people sacrificing their lives to make sure Pan didn't get it."

Stinky lifted his head. "A great sacrifice it's," he agreed. He had never believed in magic before, but with everything that had happened, he couldn't argue with it any longer. Portals, fairies, magic watches…What could possibly be next?

Poof! Suddenly, a plume of smoke emerged from behind the group, taking them all by surprise. Scrambling for their swords, my men stood tall and squinted their eyes, hoping to see who or what had caused it.

"Well, well, well… It's been a long time, hasn't it, Lily?" came a dark voice. "Did you miss me?"

The smoke cleared, revealing Pan and a few of his fairy bodyguards all standing in a row. Hearing a commotion, the rest of Tiger Lily's people quickly appeared from behind the furthest wall. Their faces were a mask of great anger, their bows expertly strung tight with the promise of deadly arrows.

They quickly flooded the room, taking their place behind Tiger Lily in a protective stance.

"Not at all, Pan. It's always a bad day when I see a face like yours." Tiger Lily's eyes narrowed, glaring daggers at Pan. She would kill him with her bare hands if she could. That was clear to everyone in the room.

Pan snorted, disgust enveloping his face almost instantly. "You should be so lucky," he said darkly. Quietly, he walked to her side, his bodyguards blocking her people from intervening.

Tiger Lily's group continued to aim their arrows his way, targeting his heart.

If he had one, that's. Even I had begun to wonder about that.

"Unfortunately, your day is about to get a lot worse," he continued. His smile was deadly, his sharp teeth seeming to stretch from ear to ear. "You see," he began with a flick of his wrist, causing a strange powder to slowly leak out. It floated into the air, quickly enveloping all of Tiger Lily's people.

They all dropped to the ground instantly, what I assumed to be some sort of magic fairy dust causing them to fall and lie sleeping. Tiger Lily stood alone with my men facing Pan and his winged minions.

"We seem to have a very big problem on our hands," he said, his voice taking a deadly turn.

"I know you gave him the clock, Lily. And I know you're smart enough to realize I would be coming." While that revelation stunned Stinky and the rest of her men, Tiger Lily didn't seem surprised. Instead, she gave a small smile, her eyes playful with her reply.

"That's true," she agreed. "I knew you would be coming, just as I knew James would be coming as well."

"So, you have been learning," Pan murmured, his eyes flickering with excitement.

"My people are capable of many different things now, Pan. You cannot imagine how far we have come since you left." Tiger Lily's eyes darkened, a warning meant to unease Pan and his fairies.

"Where did he go, Lily? Tell me now and I promise not to harm your people," he promised. We all knew better, however. There was no reason to believe he would leave them unharmed.

"If only you had shown up a few hours ago," she said cockily. "Such a shame. I don't know where he went, dear Pan. And I wouldn't tell you even if I did." She smiled and winked. "But he is already gone so there is nothing you can do about it," she finished.

Pan's eyes darkened, the black pools returning once again. The veins in his forehead throbbed, and the tendons in his arms stuck straight out as his fists clenched in anger. He wasn't very good at controlling his emotions it seemed, his body a clear giveaway.

"That's where you are wrong," he hissed. His hand disappeared behind his back, grabbing something he could use as a weapon. His fairy guards continued to hold back my men with their magic as Pan pulled a knife from his back pocket.

Tiger Lily gasped, suddenly afraid of the monster she had grown to despise over the years. She had thought she was safe in here, but the powerful fairy dust he carried seemed to have somehow broken the protection spell.

"You're going to kill me?" she guessed. "Just like you killed my parents."

"Of course not," Pan assured, his smile growing wicked once again. "Not yet, at least," he mused. "But we both know Ace will return for his men, and when he does, he'll discover I've taken you."

"He doesn't need me anymore. Taking me will do nothing but harm my people," Tiger Lily pleaded.

"Ah, we both know that isn't true!" Pan screamed, his anger roaring to life. "He tries to help every soul he encounters. He even tried saving mine. Once he knows you're gone, he'll have no choice but to feel responsible. Your people will beg for him to come save you." Pan laughed. "And when he does, he will fight me but fail. I will take back my watch, killing him once and for all," he proudly announced, turning to my men.

"No!" Stinky screamed, elbowing past one of the smaller fairy guards. He wasn't quick enough, however, as another guard stepped in his way. He raised his hand, blowing a small pile of fairy dust directly into Stinky's face. In a matter of seconds, he was on the floor snoring as loudly as the stormy sea.

Pan laughed, grabbing his belly at the sight of all the people on the floor. They had given a valiant effort as always, but it never seemed to be enough. He had always managed to beat them when it came to magic and skill.

"You will regret this," Tiger Lily warned. "You may not think much of all of us but you will be defeated one day soon, that I'm sure of."

But Pan just continued to laugh, confident he would always have the upper hand. "This has all been so fun," he drawled, placing the knife to Tiger Lily's neck. "But we really need to be going now."

The rest of my crew watched from various paralyzed angles as another plume of smoke appeared, quickly engulfing Pan and Tiger Lily. The fairy guards followed suit, leaving them all alone with the sleeping natives.

***

Back in the wild, wild west...

We set up camp later that night after parting ways with Hopalong and his brother Butch Cassidy. They had gifted us with the horses to get us through the rest of our journey, warning us to keep our eyes open because the sheriff might be on our tails.

"Take turns sleeping," he told us. "It's the safest way to assure he won't find y'all."

As we laid our beds beneath the stars, a deep voice broke the silence.

"I'll take the first shift," Hanzel offered. I had finished building a fire with Smee just minutes ago, lighting it with matches from our supplies.

I quickly nodded my head, accepting the gracious offer. I was dead on my feet, the last few days catching up with me. "Wake me up in a few hours and I'll take the next shift," I suggested. "That way Smee can get a full night's rest."

Gone was the boy who tossed and turned at night. Smee was now notoriously known for being the biggest beast in the sea when he didn't get a proper night's rest.

"Aye, aye." Hanzel winked.

I quickly made my bed, climbing into what Hanzel called a sleeping bag. It was very warm and came in handy as the desert wind began to nip at my ears. Smee had already done the same, his quiet snores echoing in the air.

I had intended to come up with a plan for what we should do next. We had to figure out how to get to Barrie and how exactly the clock worked.

But before I knew it, I had drifted off, letting sleep carry me away.

"Hook!" Hanzel whispered harshly in my ear later that night. I quickly jumped up, the sleeping bag falling to the ground. I rubbed my eyes to clear away the sleep and grabbed my sword from my scabbard.

"What is it?" I asked. My first thought was that Pan had found us once again. But when I checked my pocket for the clock, it didn't glow in warning.

"The sheriff and his men, they're just over the hill," he said frantically, pointing in the direction he came from. "We have to go."

"Grab your things and load the horses," I commanded. "Smee, wake up! Our adventure continues!"

Smee quickly emerged from his bed. In a matter of minutes, we were all ready to go, our ankles grazing the bellies of our new-found transportation.

"There they are!" The sheriff's voice boomed in the air, commanding his men to give chase in our direction. "I don't care if they're dead or alive, boys! As long as I have their bodies, I'll be a happy man!"

We swiftly goaded our horses into reaching top speed. The wind whipped by our faces as their hooves carried us away. The group of men didn't give up easily, quickly gaining on us as the sun began to rise. *It hadn't taken but a few hours for them to find us*, I thought, as Butch Cassidy's warning echoed in my mind.

"You can run, but you can't hide out here!" came the sheriff's taunting voice. "The wild west is my territory, you'll see. I know every nook and cranny."

I could hear several loud clicks as their guns began to fire, bullets ricocheting off the ground. We weaved our way through the desert, the strange dried weeds appearing once again.

We had just rounded a ridge when the ground gave way to an empty canyon below. The drop must have been hundreds of feet, the gap about a ship's length apart.

"There's nowhere to go now. You might as well surrender before I let my men kill you!" The sheriff's amused voice broke the silence. He laughed, obviously confident the chase would soon end.

But I refused to slow down, commanding my horse to go faster instead. "We can make it across to the other side," I said to Hanzel and Smee. "The canyon isn't large. We should be able to do it!"

Smee turned in my direction, a wild look in his eyes as his horse struggled to keep speed with mine. "Are you a fool?" he yelled. "There is no possibility of us making that jump! Surely we'll die!"

It was probably true, of course, but my instincts made me feel otherwise. "Just trust me on this, Smee. We can make it." I looked him dead in the eye as we raced through the night, running for our lives.

Taking a deep breath, Smee nodded his head. We grabbed our reigns, my hook held tight to the saddle horn.

"Let's do this, boys," Hanzel agreed. He looked about as confident as Smee but he, too, refused to slow down as we neared the edge.

It was soon clear that our transportation had figured out our intent. The horses began to skid and slide as they tried to slow down, disobeying our commands. They had realized there was danger ahead and tried to stop, but their hooves were not quite strong enough. My confidence suddenly disappeared as another bullet pierced the ground.

Our screams filled the air as we tumbled over the edge, certain death teasing us below. I had begun to think that we weren't going to make it, that our journey was about to end much sooner than we thought.

My instincts were quickly proving to be wrong.

As we began our freefall, my heart dropping as gravity forced us down, the clock in my pocket started to glow. I reached inside to grab it out, hoping with all of my heart that we were about to be saved.

My instincts screamed once again, causing me to quickly grab Hanzel and Smee. I locked arms with them as we continued to descent, the dusty ground only seconds away.

The clock suddenly exploded with light, blinding us all as we were once again sucked through. The deadly canyon was suddenly replaced with giant stars and moons flying past at light speed. Before we could even catch our breath, we were shot out of the portal once again. This time landing back on the Sea Devil, which we had learned to call home many years ago.

"Hook!" came Mullins frantic voice. "We've been looking for you for days!"

Confused, I turned to my crew. Stinky and the other men who had accompanied us to the temple were still not there. *But why is the ship so far away from the island?* I thought.

"Where are we?" I asked. "And why have you abandoned the plan? You were to stay anchored by the island to wait for our return." My men never made mistakes. Something like this had to have an explanation.

"As soon as you got to the island, something happened," Mullins explained. "The fog returned, blocking our view completely. It was ominous, thicker than any fog we have encountered before. It lasted only a few minutes, but once it cleared, we realized we weren't near the island anymore."

The rest of the crew looked lost as Mullins relayed the events that had played out while we were gone. While they had been told of a few magical things, this was their first experience being personally tricked by Pan.

"The fog must have carried you away," Hanzel murmured. "Pan must have had his fairies create the clouds to trick them into leaving Neverland," he stated, turning in my direction. "The same way Tiger Lily explained that he tricked us before he waged war on this ship."

"We have to get back to the temple. Stinky and the rest of our men are still there. Maybe when we get there, Tiger Lily can help us find the way to Barrie," Smee offered.

"But that means we have to get back to Neverland," Hanzel explained. "How do we do that?"

It knows where you need to go and when the time will be. Don't worry about that, Tiger Lily's voice echoed in my head.

A storm was brewing toward the west, the angry waves already beginning to rock the boat. And just like that, I had an idea. "Everyone, grab on to the ship! Don't let go until I tell you!" I commanded.

Hanzel and Smee both grabbed the rail that led below deck, the rest of my men scrambling for whatever piece closest to them.

"What are we doing?" Smee asked, curiosity lacing his voice.

"Tiger Lily said that this clock will take us wherever we need to go," I explained, the clock still grasped firmly in my hand. I tucked it in my pocket as I grabbed the wheel, steering the ship right for the storm.

"I don't think she meant we should go straight into a storm," Smee said, realizing my direction.

"It's activated by danger," I continued. "It's the only way we'll make it back to Neverland. If I can steer the ship directly into a wave, the clock will realize I'm in danger. It'll activate and take all of us back to the island."

Hanzel shook his head, a giant smile covering his face. "He's right," he agreed. "While it does seem crazy and dangerous, it's the only way."

We were entering the storm now, the waves growing in height. Rain began to pelt us all, causing our clothes to soak through and stick to our bodies like a second skin.

"Is everyone ready?" I shouted above the thunder and lightning. While we had encountered many storms on the sea before, we had never intentionally steered into one.

The rest of my crew's faces had grown pale and grey, their knuckles white as they gripped the ship with all of their strength. "Aye, aye!" they screamed.

I turned the wheel hard, the ship groaning as it headed in the direction of a massive wave. "Hold on tight!" I screamed.

My pocket glowed as the waves grew taller, the boat tipping dangerously low. *So close,* I thought. I grabbed the clock from my pocket, holding the wheel with my hook as the wave finally crashed into the deck. Light exploded all around us, the clock sucking the whole ship through.

Splash!

I opened my eyes as the ship settled, the ocean now calm beneath us.

"Woo-ee!" Smee's boisterous voice broke the silence as I scanned the deck, making sure all of my men were intact.

"We made it." Mullins astonished voice came next. "I can't believe it, but we made it! There's the island!"

We all turned, the island lush and green, located just a few hundred feet away.

"Now let's go save our men!" I yelled.

CHAPTER TEN

"Captain!" Stinky screamed as we entered the belly of the temple. It had taken us much less time to get through the maze, as we now knew what to expect.

I raised my hook in greeting. Stinky quickly waved us over. He was busying himself by helping a few of Tiger Lily's people to their feet. As they stretched their arms and legs, I noticed them shake their heads as if they had just woken up.

"What's wrong?" I asked. I could tell from the looks on their faces that something had happened while we were gone. I looked around the room, silently assuring myself that all my men were accounted for. They were all intact, just a little shaken up.

Something didn't feel right, but I couldn't put my finger on it...

And that was when I realized someone was missing. My heart raced as terrible thoughts consumed my mind.

Where was Tiger Lily? Had she been helping her people?

"Pan found us when you left," Stinky explained regretfully. "He took Tiger Lily at knifepoint while a few of his

136

bodyguards held us back. There wasn't anything we could do." His head dropped in defeat.

I placed my hand on his shoulder, a gesture meant to comfort.

"What happened to everyone else?" I asked.

The rest of Tiger Lily's tribe had finally stood up, adjusting their weapons behind their backs. "He put us to sleep with fairy dust," one of them explained. "We had a protection spell placed on the temple, but he must have figured it out. The fairies had to have created a more powerful substance than ours."

"Please, you have to find her. Tiger Lily must be saved," another said lowly. Her brown eyes pleaded with mine, a sense of urgency written across her face.

"Yes, you must!" came another voice. "She is important to our people, and we have already lost so much since we came to Neverland."

Trying to reassure everyone in the room, I nodded my head. "Don't worry. Pan won't harm her. He's probably planning to use her to get to me. I'll find her and bring her home. That's a promise I can keep."

Tiger Lily was kidnapped because of me. Her family had risked their lives year after year in the hopes that I would eventually show up. It was only right that I brought her home safe and sound.

"How are we going to do that?" Smee whispered, trying not to alarm the rest of the tribe. "We're going to need a lot more help if we have to find Pan here. His power is unstoppable. We're greatly outnumbered."

Hanzel, upon hearing our delicate conversation, jumped in. "I think they may be able to help us," he suggested. "They've lived here for a very long time. Surely they would know someone who could help us."

The tribe's chief stepped forward. He was a tall man, standing above everyone else. His eyes were a simple brown but felt very powerful, almost like he was holding the wisdom of his many ancestors deep inside. In his right hand, he held a walking stick adorned with many different feathers. As he got closer, I noticed small carvings wrapped around its frame, among them beautiful flowers and birds in mid-flight.

"There is someone who can help you," he quietly announced, motioning for one of his people to come closer. A younger man, around thirteen years of age, immediately walked our way. "This is Flying Eagle," he declared. The young boy shook our hands, his grasp firm and precise. "He can take you to someone I believe will be of great assistance to you," the Chief explained, turning to the boy. "You know where to go?" he asked.

"Yes," Flying Eagle assured his leader. "Find the tree and take them there, follow them down to Bell."

The Chief smiled, pleased with the boy's response. I wracked my brain for places named Bell on Neverland, hoping I could figure out where we were going. Though I had not been on the island for a long time, I did learn a lot during my stay with the lost boys.

"Bell?" Smee's voice came.

"Tinkerbell," Flying Eagle said simply.

My mouth dropped, suddenly remembering the stories I had heard from Pan. He and Tinkerbell used to be very close.

"Why would Tinkerbell help us?" I asked, confused. Why would one fairy risk so much?

"That's a story only she can tell," the Chief explained. He raised his hand, signaling us to refrain from asking any more questions. "It's time. You must leave quickly, before the sun sets above. The forest is dangerous at night when Pan runs wild. He can control the animals, make them do what he wants."

"We'll do our best," I assured him as he turned and walked away.

Turning to Flying Eagle, I gestured to my crew behind me. "My men are ready to leave as soon as you are."

"Just let me grab a few items and some of our fighting men," he said excitedly. Something told me this was the first time he had been given such responsibility.

They must be training him to be a soldier, I thought to myself.

I walked back to the rest of my crew, Hanzel and Smee taking the lead. We quickly filled them in on our new plan, assuring them that wherever we were going would be beneficial to the quest.

"We weren't sure what to expect," Hanzel explained. "We know only that Tinkerbell is a fairy who can help us with Pan."

"We must follow Flying Eagle and a few of the Chief's men through the forest to get to her," Smee finished.

Stinky and the rest of the crew nodded, adapting to the change with ease. The pirate life often left us scrambling to adapt and change our quests, so to them, this wasn't anything new.

"There's a lot at stake here, men," I announced. "So, keep your eyes and ears open at all times. This is an island full of magic. Tricks are hidden all throughout. If you notice anything at all, speak up!"

"Aye, aye, Captain!" they screamed.

***

By the time we reached the forest, it was around midday. We had about six hours until the sun would begin to set, meaning we had that long to find Tinkerbell's tree.

"Slow down a little," came Smee's voice, talking to Flying Eagle who was about ten paces ahead. "We have to make sure everyone can keep up with our pace."

Flying Eagle slowed to a stop, an apologetic look in his eye. "I'm sorry. I'm Tiger Lily's brother, you see, so I'm in a hurry to make sure that my sister is safe," he explained.

Suddenly, it all began to make sense. The Chief had put him in charge of this quest because of his emotions toward his sister. He would be filled with anger and remorse, especially after losing his parents years ago.

That would make him a very valuable leader out here, I thought. *Nobody will want to see this through more than him.*

"That's okay," I assured. "We know you want to save your sister more than anything in the world. Just make sure we're all together, okay?" I asked nicely. "We don't want to come across anything dangerous without being able to coordinate and attack," I explained, giving him an encouraging smile.

"I will keep that in mind," Flying Eagle promised, taking the lead once again at a much more reasonable pace.

"He's been through a lot," Hanzel commented. We were a few paces behind, the rest of my men holding the tail end of the group. Tiger Lily's soldiers slithered through the trees unnoticed at our sides, an attempt at a surprise attack if we were to encounter trouble ahead.

"He has indeed," I agreed. "He certainly seems to be holding well though, don't you think?"

"It's amazing he carries himself so strong," Hanzel continued. "He'll be a very powerful man one day. Especially if he successfully completes today's journey."

Nodding my head in approval, I smiled at Hanzel. He had learned to read people very well over the years, but it still continued to impress me day after day.

"What do you think he meant when he said we had to go 'down' to see Bell?" Smee suddenly interrupted.

"What?" I asked him. The question had me momentarily perplexed, my eyebrows drawing down in confusion.

"Find the tree and take them there, follow them down to Bell," he recited.

I pondered the different possibilities of its meaning.

"Maybe it means we have to go down a hill?" Hanzel offered, his shoulders shrugging like he had no idea.

142

"It has something to do with some sort of tree," I thought aloud. "Fairies like to hide in trees, so maybe the tree is at the bottom of a ravine." To be honest, I had no idea either. Fairies were notorious for hiding in small places off the beaten path. They were very little so they were easily hid, meaning they could be just about anywhere in Neverland.

"Maybe it's underground?" Smee guessed.

The squawk of a crow suddenly broke the air, halting our conversation completely. That was the signal we had agreed upon before leaving the temple. The tribesmen agreed to pierce the air with the bird's cry if they noticed something was afoot.

We all halted, removing our weapons and arming ourselves for whatever dared to stand in our way.

"Scan the area," I whispered. "Use only your eyes and your ears. Don't take a step in any direction." I listened closely, straining to hear the footsteps of an enemy or the rustle of an animal headed our way. But try as I might, I couldn't hear a thing.

"Shhh," Smee whispered as one of my men struggled with a cough.

The air in front of me suddenly began to swirl, a playful smoke forming just above my head. A small body formed, a furry creature with an obnoxiously wide grin.

"Hello there," it began, its tail flicking in my direction as it jumped onto a branch.

I realized it had the body of a cat, although I had never seen one colored with brilliant purples and blues like the one in front of me. Its wide smile was filled with sharp teeth, less menacing than Pan's but not friendly enough.

"Who are you?" I questioned the strange animal.

It's smile grew, taking up more of its wide face than I ever could have imagined. Was this one of Pan's tricks? It certainly played the part.

"They call me Cheshire," it explained. "And I'm here to help guide you."

Flying Eagle stepped to our side, distrust coloring his face. "My people would have told me about you," he disagreed.

"Your people didn't know I was coming," Cheshire argued simply.

"And why should I believe that?" I asked casually. If this was Pan's work, we had to be absolutely sure we didn't fall for anything.

"Because I hate Pan just as much as you do, dear Hook," he replied. "And I will do anything I can to assure your success."

I couldn't tell if this cat was telling the truth, my instincts remaining silent as I pondered his words.

"But we already know where we're going," Flying Eagle continued. He distrusted this cat instantly. I saw it all over him. He was a young boy, however, so his instincts could be wrong.

"You have circled this spot three times since your journey began," the cat announced smugly. "Pan's bodyguards created a mirage as soon as you entered the woods. He wanted to keep you off track until it got dark."

The anger disappeared from Flying Eagle's face, leaving nothing but disbelief in its place. It did sound like something Pan would do. We could all agree on that.

"But how do you know my name?" I asked, still unsure of what to believe.

"It's foretold that you are the one to save us all," the Cheshire Cat explained. "You have finally come to destroy the evilest being on the island. The Bell brought me here from my own world to help guide you, knowing Pan's magic doesn't work on me."

Had word begun to spread throughout Neverland of my destiny in life? Did Tiger Lily's tribe reveal my plan to kill Pan, giving hope where it was greatly needed?

"We have all been waiting. Pan's magic is dangerous, with the ability to spread into other worlds if not stopped," the cat finished. His eyes suddenly turned kind, and my instincts reacted almost instantly. Whatever this creature was, he was

145

definitely telling the truth. And he was willing to risk his life to make sure I reached Pan.

"I believe him," I announced, signaling to the tribesmen in the trees to keep their weapons down. Smee and Hanzel turned to me, their shoulders dropping as fear began to leave their bodies. They would always trust my decisions, just as I always trusted their judgement.

"So, how do we get out of the mirage?" Smee asked the cat. We both knew we didn't have much time left before the sun would set.

"Close your eyes and count to three, and I shall take you away with me," Cheshire purred, his voice dipping low in a melody as he sang the words out loud.

"Just like that?" Flying Eagle asked doubtfully. He didn't fully trust this cat, but I hoped he knew he could trust me. His Chief demanded he take us to see Tinkerbell. His people's lives depended on it.

"Just like that," the cat said simply. "I promise it's not you who I want to harm."

With that final statement, Flying Eagle turned to me with a face full of determination. "Okay, let us go," he conceded.

"Hear ye, hear ye, come close my brave crew! Let us all stand together and do as the creature says!" I commanded.

My men quickly gathered around, Tiger Lily's tribesmen taking their place behind her brother.

"One," Smee began.

"Two," Hanzel echoed.

"Three!" we all yelled, the cat unexpectedly turning into dust once again.

It quickly wrapped around us all, twisting between every one of our feet. Confused, we all looked down, wondering if we had just been tricked.

"Hold on tight," the cat's voice taunted, echoing from the trees nearby.

We were all catapulted upwards, and our screams filled the sky. It was safe to say we didn't see this coming as our bodies began to fly at top speed. The Cheshire cat's boisterous laugh could be heard in the air, enjoying the screams we couldn't contain. While we had been through a lot of things over the years, being shot through the air didn't seem to be one of them.

After a few seconds of flight, we all fell. Still trying to grasp the situation, I realized we were headed straight for the forest floor.

There's no way we'll survive that fall, I thought frantically to myself.

But as we neared the ground, the smoke grabbed our waists tight, slowly lowering us down until our feet gently touched ground.

Even though we didn't hit the ground, I couldn't help but brush myself off. The experience had unnerved me a smidge, but I quickly brushed it off, making sure all my men had arrived safely.

"Here we land, your journey ahead; where Tinkerbell hides, the clue covered in red," the cat sang out once more. He gave another big smile before disappearing into the trees, his tail wrapping around the leaves as he turned to smoke one final time.

"I guess that means we're here," came Smee's voice. His face was still white, a definite side effect to our latest form of transportation.

"He is right. Her home is right here," Flying Eagle announced, gesturing to a large tree to our left.

We all turned toward his voice, noticing a small hole at the base of its stump.

"Down to see Bell," Smee whispered quietly, my ears just barely catching his words. "How do we go down?"

Flying Eagle smiled, a sudden excitement crossing his features. "This is the best part," he enthusiastically replied.

Bending down, he retrieved a large piece of cake. It had been decorated in bright red frosting, delicate white letters spelling out EAT ME as a fine gold dust covered the edge.

"What are we supposed to do with that?" Hanzel asked curiously.

"Well, eat it, of course," I replied smugly.

Hanzel quickly rolled his eyes, a small smile playing on his lips. "Thank you, Captain Obvious," he said with a laugh. "But what does it do?"

Without a word, Flying Eagle took a bite, disappearing before my eyes. I blinked, scrambling to see where he had gone.

"Down here," came a muted yell.

I looked down, shocked to see he had shrunk to the size of a mushroom. The rest of his tribe took turns taking a bite, shrinking before our eyes as we stared in disbelief.

"It's the only way to get inside," he explained. "You must eat the cake."

I turned to my men, thankful I had left part of the crew on the ship. If we all had to share the cake, we wouldn't have had enough to go inside.

"You first," Smee said amused. "It's the only time you'll be smaller than me. I've got to enjoy it while I can!" He laughed.

Rolling my eyes, I took a finger full of cake, leaving just enough for the rest of my men. As I swallowed my bite, my body began to tingle, starting in my toes and stretching all the way to my head.

In the blink of an eye, my scenery changed. The tree had become giant, my body now the size of a leaf. I looked at Hanzel and Smee as they took their bites and dropped to the ground beside me.

"Whoa," Smee said, his eyes as wide as I had ever seen.

"That was intense," Hanzel agreed. In another few moments, all my men were as small as us.

"Are you ready?" Flying Eagle asked me, ignoring their comments entirely. He must have done this many times as he looked calm as could be.

"We're ready," I assured. "Lead the way."

He smiled, telling the rest of his tribe to go on ahead. "We just have to walk up these stairs," he explained as we entered the hole in the tree.

"And then we'll get to see Tinkerbell?" I confirmed.

"Yes, of course." He nodded.

My heart raced with adrenaline as we climbed the steps, becoming louder and louder as we neared the top.

"Almost there," Smee commented excitedly.

We took the last steps in silence. As I contemplated what to say, I finally laid my eyes upon Bell. I had no idea where to begin, so many questions had remained unanswered.

"Bell!" Flying Eagle screamed as we entered the fairy base. "It has finally happened!"

A small fairy in a lime green dress flew around the corner, a playful smile on her lips. Her wings batted quickly, causing a quiet buzz as she hovered. Her blonde hair was wrapped in a bun. Her blue eyes connected with the young boy.

"Quiet down, boy! Some of the fairies are sleeping," she scolded. "What on Neverland are you talking about?"

"Hook-Man has finally come like the story has foretold," he whispered, an apologetic look crossing his face. It was very important for fairies to get a good night's rest in order for their magic to be most effective.

Tinkerbell's face went slack, her mouth dropping as she stared me down.

"Well, where are my manners?" she exclaimed, embarrassed. "Please, come in. Take a seat wherever you would like. We have been waiting for your arrival."

Thanking her, we all stepped forward, their entire base now revealing itself. Long staircases weaved up and down the trunk, rooms poking out at each level. A few fairies soared above our heads as we were seated in the corner of the wide room. There was a big, square table standing out in the middle of the space; chairs scattered around its edge.

"It might be best if we sat here," I suggested. It looked like the perfect spot to have a discussion. My gut told me Tinkerbell would have a lot to say.

"Absolutely," she agreed.

We all took a seat, leaving a spot for the fairy at the head of the table. She thanked our kindness, her wings stopping as she landed softly on her little feet.

"Where to begin?" she mused.

"Why don't you start from the beginning?" Hanzel offered. "Whatever you think will help us with Pan."

When she looked at me once again, I smiled, encouraging her to continue.

"I have known Pan for a long time," she began. "We used to be very close to each other, practically spending every day together." Her smile quickly disappeared. "I had thought Pan was doing a good thing when he began to collect our fairy dust," she said, rolling her eyes. "I was so naïve, of course. He had told me he was doing it so that he could protect Neverland from its enemies. I believed him almost immediately."

152

Shaking her head, she continued her story. "But then fairies began to disappear," she explained. "At first, Pan wrote off their absence as a reward for good behavior. If we could collect as much fairy dust as they did, we could have a break as well."

Her tiny fists clenched, a reaction I had grown used to seeing when people talked about their time with Pan. "One night, I discovered the truth," she said, her voice dropping low. "I was flying around the perimeter of Pan's home, a job we all shared as fairies in his group, when I saw something not quite right down below. There had been a disturbance in the ground, the dirt scattered in a small mound about the size of a log. I quietly flew low, landing as close as I could," she said, her face turning pink.

"Please, continue," I pleaded, wondering where this story would go next.

Taking a deep breath, she foraged ahead. "As I pawed at the dirt with my bare hands, I had the worst feeling in my heart. I just knew something was wrong." Bell sniffed, a small tear escaping her beautiful eyes. "I discovered the missing fairies, their bodies left to rot in the middle of the forest. He killed them all and lied to the rest of us to cover his tracks."

I watched as Tinkerbell wiped her eyes, anger quickly replacing her sadness. Pan had lied to me as well back then when he had said he was still close to the fairy in front of me.

"I couldn't stay there any longer," she admitted. "Not after that. So, I left that night, running into a small group of fairies. We were all afraid of Pan, recognizing his evil ways instead of the savior we had believed him to be in the beginning."

"We all fell for his tricks," Hanzel said, trying to comfort Bell during her tale. "It's nothing to be ashamed about."

"Thank you." She smiled, taking Hanzel's word to heart. "We built a life here soon after, enjoying our lives free from his chains."

Standing up from the table, she walked toward me. "And then word came our way that a new lost boy had joined his crew," she mused.

I was surprised as her story changed direction, suddenly becoming about me.

"It was you," she explained. "The first boy to escape Neverland. Your story travelled through Neverland as you achieved the impossible. You were the first to outsmart Pan's evil ways, stealing his watch and trapping him here permanently."

I smiled, never once thinking what I had done was as powerful as people made it out to be.

I did what I had to do to stay alive, I thought. *And I would do it again if given the chance.*

"But once you left, Pan grew angrier than he had ever been before. He rallied up as many fairies as he could, forming an army as powerful as the sun."

"An army to fight me?" I guessed, panicking. I wasn't ready to fight an entire army. I was barely brave enough to take on Pan, let alone an army of fairies.

"Yes," she answered. "That's why you have to learn how to defeat him as soon as you can. Now that you are back in Neverland, he is going to try as hard as he can to make sure that you don't leave."

I was at a loss for words, frozen as Bell's words replayed in my mind. I had no idea I would face such a war, but it was beginning to look like defeating Pan was going to be as impossible as it seemed.

"There is an island called Barrie." Bell's voice quickly pulled me out of my head.

"We've heard of Barrie!" Smee exclaimed. "Tiger Lily told us that we must reach Barrie to discover the key to Pan's demise."

"Very well then," she said, clapping her hands. "There is only one thing left to tell."

Curiosity getting the best of me, I anxiously gave voice to my thoughts. "What else could there possibly be? I can barely handle everything that's happened so far. What else could you possibly have to throw my way?"

The table fell silent, recognizing the uneasiness in my tone. It was hard not to get frustrated when no matter what we did, our quest seemed to be getting more and more difficult.

"Now that he has completed his army," Bell's soft voice carried on, "he has been using them to dig further and further into Neverland to collect enough fairy dust for all of his new spells."

"Like controlling animals and certain plants," Flying Eagle offered. "Rumor has it that he trained a magnificent beast to find you by the smell of your blood."

"And the tick of your clock!" Bell interjected. "He can hear the tick as you get near. You must be on the lookout for this creature wherever you go. It can be disguised as any animal but is said to be very large and dangerous."

"I've not heard about the beast," I announced to them all, my veins suddenly filling with ice.

What creature could be more powerful than Pan? I wondered. It had to be something I had never seen in my short time here. I couldn't remember anything that looked large and unnerving.

"But what is all of this doing to Neverland?" I asked, momentarily changing the subject. I couldn't handle talking about the beast now. It would have to be something I thought about later. "It can't be good," I finished.

Shaking her head, Bell's face showed a look of remorse. "It's killing Neverland," she revealed. "Which is why you have to hurry. Not just to save Tiger Lily, but to save Neverland from being completely destroyed."

I nervously looked around the table, suddenly realizing how many people were beginning to depend on me. I had not imagined my life turning out like this, a constant battle to find and kill Pan, but I didn't have any other choice.

"The watch will take us where we need to go," I said after a moment of silence. "We just have to find another storm I can steer the ship into and it'll take us straight to Barrie."

"That's a good plan," Smee commented, his strained smile pointing in my direction. He was beginning to lose doubt as well. It had been hard on us all and we were ready for it to be over.

"Aye," Hanzel agreed. "We just have to make it back to the ship to fill the rest of the men in on the plan. Then we can leave right away."

"Great!" Bell announced, her dark mood suddenly replaced with a few moments of hope. "Before you go, however, you are going to need a few things." She giggled, hurriedly flying from the room.

We sat in silence as her wings carried her to the top of the base and into a small room, which I could only assume was her own. Arms full of supplies, she hastily flew back down until she was face to face with me once again.

"Here you go," she said happily, handing me a large transparent bag. Inside were dozens of small cakes, similar to the slice we had all consumed outside.

"This will allow you to shrink again should the situation call for it." She winked. "Which it'll when you reach Barrie, of course. You must search for a rock on the island shaped like a skull. Inside the skull, you will find the key to defeating Pan."

She then handed me a jar full of a thick liquid I had never seen before.

"This is fairy juice," she explained. "Sprinkled with fairy dust, of course. This will allow you to go back to your original size once you exit the tree. Just a drop will work."

I was very grateful for her gifts, realizing I had not even considered how we would get back to normal after we had left the tree.

"Thank you very much," I said, with as much gratitude as I had. "This has helped us very much."

"You are welcome," she assured. "And good luck, Hook. We all have faith in you." Her smile seemed genuine as she said goodbye to everyone in the room and led us to the stairs as we readied ourselves to leave.

"I won't let you down," I said hopefully. I was choosing to remain optimistic about the situation, ignoring the many ways I could screw it up.

Bell closed the door as we started to descend the stairs toward the bottom of the tree. I had a lot on my mind, remaining silent as I mulled over everything we had learned.

A strange beast has the scent of my blood, I thought morosely. *That's not going to be good for us. We already have to keep our eyes out for Pan. Now a giant creature is bent on ripping me apart? Will we ever catch a break?*

As we finally reached the bottom, I grabbed the bottle of fairy juice from my pack. Stepping out into the sun, I let my men each take a drop. One by one we returned to our normal size. Tiger Lily's tribe had taken bites of the cake now and suggested staying small, claiming they would return to normal size after a few hours. We could easily carry them with us for protection.

"It's better that you save the juice," Flying Eagle explained. "In case you need it in the future since that's all you have. Besides, small can be handy." He smiled.

I graciously accepted their offer, thinking it was a wise suggestion after all.

"Just promise me that you will save my sister," he pleaded, his brown eyes filling with sadness.

"I promise," I said passionately. "If it's the last thing I shall ever do, I will return your sister to the temple unharmed."

CHAPTER ELEVEN

As we made our way back through the forest, Flying Eagle and his people stashed safely in our breast pockets, I couldn't help but feel the weight of the world on my shoulders. Just a decade ago, I was just a young man angry with his father, pleading for a better life.

With everything that's happened since, I now found myself responsible for countless lives and the existence of everything on Neverland. It all fell in the palm of my hand.

"We just have to get to Barrie and everything will work itself out," Hanzel reassured me.

"I certainly hope so," I mumbled quietly. "This has turned out to be much harder than expected, hasn't it?" I asked with a smile.

Giving a small laugh, Hanzel nodded in agreement and grinned back. "You can surely say that again. But I wouldn't have it any other way."

I couldn't help but chuckle at his answer. No matter what we got ourselves into, Hanzel always managed to remain positive. I didn't know how he did it, but it was something I hoped to learn as the years continued to pass.

"What are you two whispering about?" came Smee's curious voice. "I'm a part of this team, too, you know."

"Calm down," I encouraged. "We were only discussing that once we got to Barrie, our plan would become clear as day."

"The sooner we get there, the sooner we can defeat Pan," Hanzel insisted. We were all walking at a steady pace now, our bodies anxious to return to the ship.

"It's about time," Smee agreed wholeheartedly. "A vicious storm seems to be brewing on the island, one only we can settle down."

He was referring to the war, of course. We were all a little exhausted from our journey but couldn't let the threat of Pan and his fairy soldiers bring us down. And while it had been foretold that I was the only one capable of completing the task, I couldn't help but think none of this would be possible without Smee and Hanzel by my side.

"You are very brave men," came Flying Eagle's voice, hidden in my breast pocket below. "I hope that someday I can be just as courageous as you."

"You will be, boy," Hanzel quietly announced. "Maybe you will even be able to save us one day." He smiled as Flying Eagle's head rose above the pocket's edge.

162

The tiny boy laughed, shaking his head at the possibility. "Wouldn't that be something?" he agreed.

I had become engrossed in the conversation, momentarily forgetting the path of our surroundings. I failed to notice a tree up ahead, its sharp branches swinging low in the wind.

Smack!

My vision went fuzzy as I tumbled to the ground. One of the low hanging branches had swatted me square in the face, causing me to lose my balance. I felt Flying Eagle's shrunken hands gripping my shirt for safety, managing to stay inside my pocket as I quickly got myself together.

"Are you okay?" came Smee's frantic voice. He and Hanzel were immediately by my side, helping me step to my feet.

"It was just a little fall," I assured the group. "No need to worry."

I was a little embarrassed as I stood up, feeling less like a captain and more like the clumsy boy I used to be. Paying close attention to our surroundings was one of the first things Blackbeard had taught us when he took us under his wing.

"The smallest obstacle could cause you to lose a battle," he had said. *"Always pay attention to the world around you."*

I'd have to watch the forest more closely, I concluded. I was lucky it was such a minor fall. Next time it could prove to be fatal.

"You're bleeding," Hanzel whispered, immediately grabbing a small handkerchief from his pack.

Confused at his revelation, I brought my left hand to my face, feeling for whatever injury I had sustained. I wasn't hurting, so it must have been something insignificant.

I pulled my hand back, a thin coat of blood shining bright red on my fingertips.

"It got you right above the eye," Hanzel said, pressing the makeshift bandage to my face. "We have to get it covered up fast. Smee, check how close we're to the shore. Hurry!" he commanded.

Honestly, I didn't know why he was making such a fuss about it. I was fine, really.

"There's nothing to be upset about Hanzel. I'm okay. We'll make it to the ship without a problem," I said calmly.

"Do you not remember?" he asked incredulously. "The beast we were warned about can smell your blood. No matter how small the amount."

My skin crawled as I realized the danger we were in once again. The vicious creature could be anywhere on

Neverland, making its way in our direction as soon as it caught my scent.

I jumped to my feet, springing into action as I held the kerchief to my face. "Smee, what's the word?" I yelled.

"The ship's a few hundred paces away," he informed us, running back to our side. "The temple is just ahead, meaning we just have to make our way back through the thickets until we see the shore."

I pulled Flying Eagle from my breast pocket, setting him on the forest floor. Hanzel and Smee followed my lead, doing the same with the rest of the tribesmen.

"Go back to your temple," I instructed. "Tell the Chief we're headed to Barrie. Once we're there, we'll find the key to defeating Pan. With that, we'll be able to rescue Tiger Lily and bring her home once and for all." My words jumbled together as I told him the plan. "We have to make it out of here before the creature finds us," I explained. "But I'll return with your sister. You have my word."

Flying Eagle's eyes filled with terror, realizing the gravity of the situation. He and his men would soon return to normal size but would probably be forced to make it inside the temple in the proportions they were now.

"You'll make it," I promised. "The beast isn't after you. As small as you are, you won't even be noticed. Now, go! As quick as you can."

"Stay safe and protect each other," the boy commanded, immediately disappearing into the trees ahead as he made his way home.

"Leave the kerchief," Hanzel's deep voice instructed. "It has your blood on it. If the creature is near, it'll be distracted by the scent and come here."

I did as he said, quickly throwing it under a pile of nearby leaves. It was a good a plan as any to throw the beast off track. We then gathered our things and took off in a sprint, my heart racing with every step.

When we reached the thickets just a few minutes later, we all knew what to do. Pulling our swords from our sash as fast as we could, we chopped at the thick vegetation standing in our way. Seconds later, we reached the other side, our boots now standing on the shoreline.

"I see the ship!" Smee exclaimed excitedly. "We made it!"

"But what's that?" Hanzel asked, a different tone coloring his voice. He pointed toward the ship, his brows drawn in confusion.

I looked toward the sea, my eyes straining to find what he was referring to. I couldn't see anything on the ship but our men, waving enthusiastically as they noticed us.

I couldn't help but smile, immediately waving back. "They're excited about our arrival," I guessed.

"I don't think that's why they're waving," Hanzel warned, pointing to the ocean below.

"Help!" my crew onboard screamed, immediately disproving my assumption. They were pointing toward the water as well, frantically trying to get our attention.

Grabbing my telescope from my pack, I stretched its body taunt I urgently brought it to my left eye, scanning the water around the edge in hopes of identifying the threat.

As my eyes adjusted, I noticed a disturbance breaking the surface. A large creature with dark green scales and spikes down its back circled the ship, its deadly tail creating small waves. I didn't know it yet, but the beast had come to taunt my men in the hopes of finding me.

"It's a crocodile," Hanzel informed us. "A very large one, in fact. Bigger than any I have ever seen."

"A crocodile?" Smee said in disbelief. "It looks like a dinosaur!"

"We have to do something," I commanded. "The crocodile looks like it's trying to tip the ship over. We have to help our crew."

It continued to circle the ship. Everyone grabbed the rails on the deck as its body rocked back and forth. I pulled the telescope from my eye, collapsing it back to its original size as I slipped it back in my pocket.

"We need a distraction," Hanzel suggested. He rubbed his chin in contemplation, trying to come up with a plan to save the men.

"What kind of distraction?" Smee asked. "It's not like we can just throw a rock into the water and scare him away." He snorted.

Hanzel rolled his eyes, his hands quickly going to his hips. "I didn't mean something like that," he shot back. "But what if we can get its attention on us?"

That would get it away from the boat, I thought to myself.

"What do we do then?" I asked. "Once it's headed our way, we'll either have to defeat it or scare it off."

I wasn't exactly thrilled at the prospect of having to defeat a giant crocodile. Its scaly skin didn't look like it could be pierced by a sword, and we had decided to leave our heavy guns on the ship.

A terrible decision, really.

"I'm not so sure it can be scared off," Smee said apprehensively. He turned toward the reptile once again, shaking his head at its size. "That thing is huge."

He was right. Looking at the crocodile, it had to be half of a ship length. Whatever beasts grew that large were alive for that reason alone.

"It's faster in the water than it is on land," Hanzel said, thinking aloud. I could see the gears turning in his head.

"So, we need to get it to land," I agreed. At least then it would be away from our crew. We could figure out what to do after that.

I gulped.

At least it isn't the beast trained to kill me, I thought. *It would've turned toward the scent of my blood by now.*

Suddenly, my instincts roared to life, an idea striking me like no other. "If the clock senses my danger, it'll know to transport us back to the ship," I said. Hanzel and Smee smiled with relief, realizing the cleverness of my plan.

"We just have to get the crocodile's attention and wait for it to swim to shore. Then, once it's close enough and the clock begins to glow, I'll grab hold of you both until we land safely on the deck."

Simple as that.

"How do we get its attention?" Smee asked curiously. "It looks like it really wants to eat everyone onboard, not just us three."

"Crocodiles will go for easy or wounded prey first," Hanzel explained. "The three of us will look like an easy meal so it should immediately turn in our direction once it knows we're here."

Getting its attention would be the easy part. Something as simple as yelling would probably do. We just had to make it aware we existed.

"Prepare yourselves just in case," I warned Hanzel and Smee. "Just because we have this clock doesn't mean we're safe from danger. Now is not the time to make a mistake."

Nodding their heads, we all grasped our swords. We had a few extra knives in our packs, but everything else had been left aboard. If the clock didn't sense my danger, we were about to be in very big trouble.

"Hey!" I yelled at the big beast. "Over here!" We were all jumping up and down, waving our arms in a frantic motion.

Hanzel whistled, something I had never learned. My lips always made a smacking noise instead of a high-pitched squeal.

Smee changed his course, clapping his hands as he jumped in the air instead. We were doing whatever we could do be as loud as possible, anxiously waiting for the crocodile to turn our way.

As I let out a blood-curdling cry, a sound deep enough to carry for miles, the creature suddenly became still. The boat stopped rocking as the waves no longer formed, the croc sitting as still as stone. It seemed to have heard us but wasn't turning around.

"Do we not look tasty?" Smee screamed, teasing the creature our way. "Come and get us!"

Tick.

Pan's watch made a noise within my front pocket, momentarily catching my attention. It shouldn't be making a noise at all. Pan was nowhere near us and it didn't glow.

"It's turning," Hanzel whispered. "Headed our way."

I looked up, deciding to ignore the watch for the time being. The crocodile had finally turned around, weaving delicately through the water as it came straight for us.

Tock.

"What in the world?" I asked aloud, distracted by the watch in my pocket again. It shouldn't be making that noise. I pulled it out with my left hand, noticing that it still had not begun to glow.

There must be something wrong with it, I assumed.

"I have been waiting for you," a mysterious voice came across the sand. "I can smell you a mile off. Your scent is as delicious as dessert."

Tiny bumps covered my skin as I realized where the voice was coming from. The creature in the water had spoken! And it had caught my scent…

"It's the beast of which we were warned," Smee whispered, the blood draining from his face instantly.

"Correct," the crocodile smugly announced, his voice the most ominous I had ever heard. "But you may call me Tick."

I quickly looked at Hanzel and Smee, their faces turning toward me in terror. Our plan didn't seem so simple anymore as we were faced with another great obstacle.

"Just stick to the plan," I whispered. It was our only chance at getting out of there alive; we just had to keep our eyes on the quest. They both nodded, gripping their swords harder as the sweat beaded on their brow.

"Come here, my tasty morsel," the beast encouraged. "I just want a little bite, I promise."

The hair on the back of my neck rose as the crocodile neared the edge of the shore. It would be walking on land any minute. Whatever happened next would determine if we were to live or die. We had no choice but to count on the watch.

"So, you work for Pan," I said calmly. I was hoping to distract the beast with conversation, buying a little extra time until the watch decided to activate or glow.

Tick laughed. "I don't work for Pan," it said hotly. "I don't work for anyone."

"But he sent you, did he not?" Hanzel baited, figuring my intent. He winked in my direction to signal that he understood.

The crocodile's tail splashed angrily, water spraying us all. "I'm a creature more powerful than he," the beast said. "I have been on Neverland a very long time. I don't need Pan to survive."

"We didn't say you did," I calmly said, casually taking a few steps back. "Just that he tells you what to do." I shrugged my shoulders, my tranquil demeanor a complete mirage.

Tick snapped its mouth shut, making a cracking noise so loud it shook the ground beneath our feet. It let out a long hiss as it slowly emerged from the cold, dark sea.

"I am going to enjoy killing you, Hook. I promised to bring you back alive, but I just don't think that's possible anymore." Somehow, it had managed to smile, its long rubbery tongue licking its reptilian lips.

"I bet that's going to make Pan very mad," Smee taunted. "He'll definitely punish you for that."

The crocodile's eyes turned red, a slight glow emitting from their depths. Its deadly claws dug into the ground. It slowed down as we played with its mind, our plan quickly becoming a success.

I hooked my thumb in my pocket, taking a subtle peek in my pocket. The clock had begun to glow, the tiniest of light visible within.

"It's working," Hanzel whispered.

"He will do no such thing," the beast hissed. "I'm Tick the great croc! I do what I want and take what I please. I'm a creature of great violence. No Pan can control me!"

"But he did send you here to kill me," I said under my breath, just loud enough for it to hear me.

"So, he did kind of control you," Smee agreed. We all nodded our heads as it shook in anger. I could see how this affected the beast with the way his body went rigid. His entire back of scales glistened in the sunlight as he moved through the water, the rage in its eyes visible from the deck of the ship. Seeing this, we knew we had the upper hand. Nothing could maintain logical thought when in a blind rage, and we had aimed for just that.

The clock continued to get brighter as it took one step closer, its breathing growing more rapid. We just needed to distract it for a few more minutes. The clock would surely suck us in by then.

"I won't tell you again," Tick said, his voice as dark as the sea. "I merely offered to come get you. Pan knew I was the only one powerful enough to do so. Even he couldn't get you, so what does that mean?"

"That means he tricked you into thinking that you were more powerful than he," Hanzel said as he grinned. "Don't worry, lad. He's tricked all of us before."

The crocodile's attention suddenly switched to Hanzel, its eyes narrowing in his direction. "And I will kill you first." It smiled, turning to me. "And you will watch."

My palms began to sweat as Tick's promise ran up my spine. "You'll do no such thing," I warned.

"Did I not already tell you, dear Hook, that I do what I want?" The evil creature laughed. "Not even you can stop me. I'm too mighty!"

Unexpectedly gaining its confidence back, the crocodile took several steps forward. We all jumped back in surprise. The clock now grew bright enough to be seen through the cloth. Tick hissed as it continued to glow.

"The watch is all I need," it mocked in a voice that sounded like a snake slithering on the ground. "Pan won't care if I kill you as long as I bring that back."

It was true, of course. But I wasn't going to let that happen.

"Well, it sounds like we have a problem," I said, trying to distract him once more. "Because I don't feel like dying today." I placed my hands on my hips, shrugging my shoulders as if we had reached a stalemate.

"I do not think you have a choice," came Tick's deadly voice. He licked his lips once again, and I realized our time was almost up. He would attack any second. I had to bring his attention to me.

"If you think you are strong enough to beat me, you must prove it to me first," I goaded the beast. "Because I don't think you are better than me."

"As you wish," Tick said simply. The creature took one deep breath, seeming to target me. I tucked my sword in my sash, my only hand having to grab the clock as the crocodile drew near. My only defense would be the hook on my hand, leaving me little chance of survival.

Hanzel and Smee drew close to my side, their stance protective as they held their swords close. Whatever happened next would be a great battle, no matter the outcome.

Tick. Tick. Tick. The clock clicked as the crocodile took off in a sprint, zeroing in on my body with its poisonous eyes. It ran faster than I thought possible, quickly gaining speed as it flew across the sand.

Holding the clock firmly in my hand, I linked arms with Hanzel and Smee, praying it would take us away any second. Our arms locked tight, I watched as Tick jumped into the air without warning. It gained altitude rapidly as its jaws opened wide, revealing a mouth capable of eating me in one bite.

I closed my eyes, sure I was about to die. The clock wasn't working as fast as I thought it would, leaving us vulnerable to the beast.

"No!" Hanzel cried, shocking me enough to open by eyes back up in a hurry. I felt an immense pressure to the side, sending me flying across the shore. I landed with an *oomph*, quickly realizing I was still linked with Smee.

177

I turned to my right, expecting to see Hanzel lying on the ground beside me. The only thing I could see was a piece of driftwood that had washed up from sea, my dear friend not in sight.

The clock began to shake as it recognized the imminent danger. I turned back to the beast in the hopes that Hanzel was near enough to grab.

"Hanzel!" Smee's desperate cry pierced the air.

Tick had Hanzel by the leg, shaking him through the air. I realized we must have been pushed out of the way of the croc's attack.

The clock suddenly exploded with light. Our bodies were sucked in as we watched a part of our family sacrifice himself for the cause. My throat squeezed shut in grief, my mind unable to recognize the different worlds we passed by as we were sucked through time and space.

I cried out sharply as our bodies hit the deck, the portal spitting us out on our home. I ran to the edge of the ship, unable to stop the tears from streaming down my face. I watched in horror as Tick dragged Hanzel into the forest, his lifeless body leaving a trail through the sand.

My body shook as every sob tore my throat open. I grabbed onto Smee, his face full of remorse as he realized we had just experienced the greatest loss of our lives.

"He sacrificed himself for us," he sobbed into my shoulder. "It should have been me! It could have been me!"

We had grown to love Hanzel with all our hearts over the last years. I had grown closer to him than my own father, and Blackbeard as well. I had never felt a pain such as this. It felt like my heart was being ripped right out of my chest, leaving my body raw.

"I know," I whispered to Smee. "His death must not be in vain. We must defeat Pan now more than ever and avenge his soul by killing the crocodile as well. They'll both feel the wrath of my fury, just as it was foretold!"

We both cried as the crew rushed our way, Mullins the first one to arrive. "There's a storm approaching, Captain!" he cried.

I turned to my men. Tears stained my skin. The loss of our fallen brother was a devastating moment in time. Although we had lost many before, this would prove to be the most difficult of all.

"Head straight for the storm," I choked out. "We're headed to Barrie. We must put ourselves in the path of danger again so that the clock will take us there."

Mullins nodded in understanding, sadness painting across his face as well. All the men would take Hanzel's death just as they had with Blackbeard. Melancholy would plague us all as we came to terms with another lost family member.

Starkey stepped forward, wringing his hat between his hands. "He was one of the best men I have ever met," he said simply, nodding to himself in agreement. "He will be greatly missed." And with that, he stepped away to help Mullins set sail north.

I would now do whatever it took to kill Pan. Even if I had to sacrifice my life, I would be the cause of his demise. I had never felt this level of rage before, I realized, as it danced through my veins.

The ship began to turn as another crew member announced it would be about an hour before we reached the storm.

"We won't fail now," I assured Smee. "Pan must be stopped before the rest of Neverland is destroyed. Too many people have died for us to turn back."

"I know," Smee agreed as he wiped the snot from his nose. "I'll do whatever it takes to take him down." The tears in his eyes belied his deep rage.

We both stood in place, momentarily pulling ourselves together. We would both cry later, I was sure, but just then we had a friend to avenge.

"Prepare yourselves for battle," I addressed my men. "Today, one of our best men sacrificed himself to save his Captain. Do you all know why?" I asked.

"Because you are the Captain!" Starkey yelled.

"Not quite," I replied. "There's more at stake here than we ever could have imagined. Word has it that Pan has created an army, specifically meant to defeat us all. He's harvesting fairy dust deep within the heart of Neverland, threatening the very existence of this world," I explained.

"We have to be ready to fight harder and stronger than we have before," Smee said. He now stood by my side, my second-in-command now that we were a team of two.

"We'll be facing a great deal of evil after we take the next step of our journey," he finished.

The men stood silent for a few seconds, digesting the words.

"What does that mean?" came Mullin's quiet voice.

What does it mean? I asked myself.

"It means war," I announced to the crew.

CHAPTER TWELVE

As the ship changed direction, its bow now facing North, I took a moment to collect myself in Blackbeard's old room. I closed the door and removed my hat, throwing it onto the bed. Today had been the worst day of my life by far, but we still had a long way to go.

Once we got to Barrie, we would have to scour the island until we found the rock shaped like a skull. I was hoping it could be seen by the island's edge, but I wasn't going to hold my breath for such luck.

I had just sat down when there came a knock at the door. I sighed, already knowing who it was.

"Come in, Smee," I said.

Slowly, the door opened, and Smee stepped inside. His face was defeated, and I knew he was feeling just as guilty as I was.

"How are you feeling?" he asked.

"I'm not feeling great," I admitted. "But I can't let that get in the way of what we've all been working so hard for." I shook my head, bile rising in my throat as I once again pictured Hanzel's body being dragged away.

He didn't even get a proper burial like we had done with Blackbeard.

"I just can't stop thinking about it," Smee whispered. He was staring at the wood on the ground, his eyes glazed over with sadness. "It should have been me."

"Silence!" I quietly commanded. He raised his head, surprise replacing the sorrow he wore like a mask.

"I will never hear those words spoken by you again," I continued. "Hanzel chose our lives over his. It wasn't a decision for you to make. You can't let yourself be consumed by the events that occurred. I'll miss him just as you will, but Hanzel would want us to continue on our path. We'll avenge his soul together; do you hear me?"

Although it felt like my heart had been ripped from my chest, I still had to be captain out here. I couldn't let the death of Hanzel blind me with grief until I lost sight of what mattered most. He gave his life so that I could defeat Pan. I had no choice but to follow through.

"I hear you, Captain," Smee said quietly. His fists clenched at his sides as he looked directly into my eyes.

"But I'll be the one to kill the crocodile." His voiced suddenly dropped as his eyes melted into pools of hot lava. "While you're busy killing Pan."

Smee's sudden change of behavior rendered me unable to speak for a few seconds. I had never seen him this vengeful before.

"That's a promise I can make," I finally said. "You'll be the one to defeat Tick while I finally bring down Pan."

I smiled, assuring Smee they would meet the same demise they had inflicted upon Blackbeard and Hanzel.

"If it's the last thing we do," Smee agreed. "They would do the same for us."

"Aye, that they would," I said softly. If the tables were turned, they would be doing just the same. There were too many people in danger to just leave. Neverland had to be saved, and the rest of Pan's soldiers needed to know the evil he had become.

"So, what's the plan once we reach Barrie?" Smee asked, changing the subject. Our moment of grief was now over. We had urgent matters to discuss.

"We find the formation Bell described to us. That's all I know. Depending on the size of the island, we may be able to see it from the ship. If we can't, we'll have to walk around the island until we find where it stands," I said simply. "Of course, we'll all be armed more carefully." I scratched my chin, thinking. "For we don't know what creatures may come our way."

If life had taught me anything so far, it would be that no matter where I seemed to go, I always ran into some kind of danger. And I *always* felt unprepared.

"Guns would be wise." Smee smiled. He had been practicing his shooting over the years and was getting very good. Before the night we met, he had never even laid his eyes upon a gun before. Now, he was a very skilled shooter.

I chuckled, nodding. I wouldn't argue if Smee wanted to bring his gun. Whatever weapons he chose would be the right choice for him. He grew more confident every day and I knew his instincts were becoming strong.

"Well, I should go gather my things," Smee said, turning back toward the door. "We must be about halfway to the storm by now."

I grabbed my hat, putting it back on. I decided to go back out to the deck for an update from Mullins and the crew, so I followed Smee out the door.

"Captain." Mullins nodded as I walked his way. He stood at the wheel, keeping the ship on course.

"What's the word?" I asked. "Are we near?"

"Very," he informed. "Although the waves are much less violent than they should be." Mullins looked confused as he looked out at the sea.

I turned toward the storm as I noticed the ship had barely begun to rock back and forth. The clouds were black like smoke, headed straight for us. Fog had begun to roll in over the water's edge, and I watched lightning strike its tip.

Those were all signs of a great storm, so I couldn't comprehend why the waves were as calm as could be.

"That's unusual," I murmured. "I don't think I've seen a storm such as this."

Maybe the water got choppy further ahead, I said to myself. There was no way the sky would be so deadly while the water moved calmly below.

Quiet humming suddenly filled the air, serenading my men all at once. It was a beautiful sound that entered my ear, making me curious about the source. It sounded like it was coming from the sea.

"That's the most beautiful thing I've ever heard," Starkey said dreamily. His eyes shuttered closed as he walked to the edge of the ship, a big smile on his face.

The humming got louder until I recognized its melody.

"Come closer, come closer, my dear pirate men. Come closer for we cannot see. We have something to tell you, my dear pirate men. There is treasure down here in the sea."

I couldn't help but close my eyes as the rhythm of these beautiful singers carried me away. My boots smacked the deck as I made my way to the starboard side. I had no control of my actions, my body deciding for me.

"Come closer, come closer, my dear pirate men," they sang in a whisper. *"Come closer to this siren song. We have something to show you, my dear pirate men. There is treasure and we're not wrong."*

Our bodies leaned simultaneously over *Sea Devil's* rails. We were captivated by the sweet sound in the air like a magnet pulled us close.

I leaned over the edge and caught sight of the songstresses below. They had beautiful faces that looked like porcelain and their skin seemed to be glowing in the fog. I focused on the one nearest to me as she swam just a few feet away.

"My name is Hook," I muttered dumbly. "And you are the loveliest girl I have ever seen."

She has to be freezing, I thought to myself.

"Come aboard!" I yelled without thinking.

I had never let a stranger aboard the ship because it was too much of a risk to the crew. But today, without hesitation, I

187

was asking what looked to be about twenty women to come aboard.

My gut tingled in alarm.

"That's okay, dearest Hook. I'm perfectly okay," she assured me with a smirk on her face. "Why don't you take a dip in the water? It's calm as could be. We have treasure to show you and your men. Jump in!"

For a second, I considered diving right in. I was contemplating taking my boots off when I realized what she had just said.

"Stop!" I yelled to my men. They all froze, some of them halfway over the rails as they all prepared to follow these beautiful women away.

"How do you know my name?" I demanded.

I had quickly regained use of my body as my instincts told me what tricks I had almost fallen for. These were not friendly women singing songs in the sea. They were mermaids sent by Pan to distract me from reaching the storm ahead.

I swallowed hard as the mermaids revealed their true form. Gone were the bright eyes that sparkled like the stars in the sky, only to be replaced by a glowing orange hue, similar to that of a raging fire. Their teeth sharpened, like the evil creatures we had met before, and their tongues grew long like a fork. These were not normal mermaids. These were the worst kind of mermaids... sirens. Sent to lead men to their deaths so they could feast on them.

"Your men are not as weak as I expected," the mermaid in front of me admitted. "But that doesn't mean you are not still coming with me."

"I'm afraid I can't do that." I shrugged, signaling for my men to grab their weapons. Mermaids were not hard to fight once you overcame their song spell.

"You caught us at a bad time really, you see. We were just about to leave," I explained. I wanted to get this over with quickly so that we could get to Barrie already.

"We were sent by Ariel to bring you back, I'm afraid. You are not going anywhere," she hissed. The air began to buzz around me as I noticed a soft flapping noise from above.

Who is Ariel? I asked myself. *And what would she want with me?*

"If you don't come with us," she continued, "we'll have no choice but use deadly force, and I can assure you that you will like that even less." The surrounding mermaids laughed, a cackle so off putting the hairs on my body stood stiff.

They were creepy, sure, but they didn't stand a chance against my crew. I didn't understand why she was so confident in taking us with her. She had to know her mistake.

"Whoever this Ariel is, she can wait. I have more pressing matters to attend to," I tried to say politely.

The buzzing grew louder, and I realized we were about to enter the storm. The fog had gotten thicker than before, the clouds above spitting drops of cool rain down my arms. I sighed in relief as the beads wet my clothes and stained the wood beneath my feet.

But there are still no waves, I worried to myself. *How would we get Tiger Lily's clock to transport us to Barrie if we aren't in danger?*

"You are such a fool." The mermaid below laughed. "We're not alone out here. Ariel sent us with a few extra girls just in case you were clever enough to fall out of our spell."

I rolled my eyes at the mermaid's warning. Bringing more mermaids into the fight wouldn't do a thing. They couldn't walk on land but for ten days a year when their tails temporarily turned into legs. They couldn't come on deck without legs, of course, so they were no danger to anyone aboard.

"Ladies!" she called, a smug look on her face as her tongue slithered in and out of her mouth.

To my surprise, I noticed movement coming from the sky as lightning illuminated their figures. I recognized their kind immediately, failing to be the mermaids I had assumed. Instead of the minor creatures that swam in the sea, I watched as a group of fairies lowered themselves onto the deck of the *Sea Devil*.

"Do you recall a glowing mermaid standing on two legs, with hair as red as a rose?" the lead fairy asked. She had spiky white hair and a yellow dress on that sparkled with fairy dust as she danced her tiny, lithe feet straight to me.

I thought back to the times I had seen mermaids up close during my ten years at sea. It had been only a handful of experiences that I could recall. And red hair wasn't something I could remember from those times...

"On Pan's ship," she hinted.

It took those three words to trigger my brain, remembering the young girl standing on Pan's vessel the same day he had taken Blackbeard's life.

I had barely noticed her at the time and I surely didn't believe she was a mermaid. "But she stood with two legs on that ship's deck," I argued. "How can she be a mermaid if it's not their ten sacred days?"

"She is a special mermaid," the fairy said with her hands on her hips. "She walks and she swims any day she wants. And she works closely with Pan.".

"We won't go with you," I announced, a warning in my eye for my men.

It said ready yourselves because we were about to get into another sticky situation. If they were truly here because of Pan, they wouldn't leave us alone without a fight.

The rain had begun to fall at a quicker pace now. It pelted the hat on my head and dripped from the tip of my sword. The boat swayed some as the storm gained a little power, the waves turning into the size of small hills.

"Oh, but you will," the fairy countered as her wings began to flap again, lifting her above the sail of my ship. "We have a spell," she continued, "that will allow us to bring all of you back to Pan, so you can pay for the things you have done."

Her eyes were accusatory. I recalled the things everyone had been told about me. They saw me as a traitor and an enemy of Neverland because I had been the one abusing the soil. It was dying because of the choices I had made; therefore, I must be killed for my sins.

"I didn't do the things you think I've done," I pleaded with the fairies. They must have learned the spell directly from Pan, as it didn't exist in the years past.

"Don't lie to me!" the yellow fairy screamed as lightning struck the water again. All the fairies had gathered in a circle. They held hands and rocked from side to side.

192

"I'm not lying!" I screamed in defense as panic rose. I had to think of a plan fast, before we were taken away.

Smee ran to my side as I wracked my brain for anything that would save us. We weren't ready to fight Pan. We needed to get to Barrie first.

"We could make waves with the boat," he whispered in my ear frantically. "We just have to run from side to side to make it tilt with our weight."

I smiled at Smee's plan, thinking it was the smartest idea he had in years. I was as proud as I imagined a father would be.

"Sneak around to each man. Tell him exactly what you told me," I instructed my second-in-command. "When I give you the signal of wiping my brow, run to the starboard side first. We have to be quick to beat the fairies before they finish their spell."

"Aye, aye." He slinked away. He was sneaky enough to slide through without being seen. The fairies were still distracted above. This was probably their first time trying out the spell, so it would take a little more time.

I needed to keep their attention on me. "I have one more question," I announced to them all. "What would I have to gain from destroying Neverland?"

The fairies turned back to me, their faces a mixture of confusion and anger as they processed my words. I needed to stall.

"It doesn't matter," one concluded, turning to the other girls. "Pan said he is a danger to us all, so we must do what he says to keep our people safe."

My crew was all informed now as Smee turned to the last man aboard. They all stared straight at me, waiting for the signal.

As they nodded their heads like their minds were made up, I wiped my brow as a signal to the men. Smee led the way as they ran to the rail, causing the boat to dip low with their weight.

"What are you doing?" the yellow fairy demanded.

"Just getting some exercise. Don't mind us." I smiled up at them, sweeping my hand in dismissal. The ship rocked harder as the men made their way to the other side.

"Stop it!" she shrieked.

I didn't reply as they reformed their circle and began to chant the spell. It was in a language I had never heard before, something they must have recently created.

He taught his army a special language? I thought as we managed to get the ship's side to touch the water with our next run. It would take just a few more times now to get it rocking

194

hard enough to flip. I looked at my pocket as we turned around, getting ready to go once again. Tiger Lily's clock had begun to shine, an alarm that danger was nearby.

"It's working," I said astonished. I couldn't believe we were powerful enough to blow this thing over. We were going to have to find a new ship soon if we kept getting ourselves into these kinds of situations. I was surprised it had held up so far.

"Don't give up men!" I yelled as the fairies' chant grew louder, their language still unrecognizable to my ear.

Water sloshed onto the ship with our next turn, the ship groaning loud in protest. I had guessed it would only take one more run until the danger became extreme. The clock now shined bright, lighting up the deck in the fog as sprinted once again to the rail.

Dammit! I thought as water once again splashed the deck. Unfortunately, we didn't begin to flip over, the ship proving to be stronger than I thought.

The air buzzed once again as the fairies hummed a song, hinting they were nearly done with the spell. We had only one more chance to make it work before their magic would take us unwillingly to Pan.

We charged ahead one last time, screaming out loud as we pushed our legs down. We were exhausted by now as it required a lot of power to make a ship this heavy tip over.

195

Tiger Lily's clock detonated with light as our bodies rocked the ship enough to flip. We all grabbed hands and wrapped our legs around the rails. I took a deep breath just before my face hit the water, the cold shocking my body like lightning.

As I ran out of breath, we were sucked into the clock, away from the fairies and their strange language.

We made it! I thought as the universe sped by.

The ship plopped onto water once again, right side up, a loud splash echoing in the air. "Is everyone alive?" I yelled, praying all my men had arrived.

"Aye, Captain! There is no lost soul on this ship," Smee assured me, his smile almost blinding. He looked like a little boy once again.

"Have we made it?" I asked, turning toward the island.

As I caught sight of Barrie once and for all, my chest expanded with joy. We had worked so hard to get here and lost so much.

"We must get to land!" Smee said excitedly. "Mullins, load the dinghy! We need all of the weapons you can fit."

Minutes later, we had packed ourselves into the small boat, Mullins and Starkey sitting in front of me and Smee. We decided on only four men for now. We had flares in our pack to signal if we needed more men to come ashore, something Hanzel had taught us. We were hoping there was no danger on the island but were armed with guns and swords just in case.

"I have another good feeling," Smee commented as we raced across the green water. It was a stunning color, unnatural and somehow crystal clear.

"I do, too," I agreed as we made it to shore, the cool breeze making it a perfect temperature.

"Today proves to be a good day," Starkey commented, staring straight at the sun. His eyes were closed as he soaked it in.

"It does mark a special day," I said quietly, more to myself than anyone.

"What special day?" Smee asked as he scooped water from the side of the small boat and poured it straight into his mouth.

"A day we'll all remember," I began with a smirk. "Because today is the beginning of the end for Peter Pan."

CHAPTER THIRTEEN

As our dinghy neared the front of the island, I decided to take a closer look. Across the land stood large, jagged rocks. They rose tall above the lush trees that covered the ground, their sharp points sticking out from the leaves.

I couldn't see a formation that looked like a skull as I peeked at each group of visible rocks. It must be somewhere hidden on the island within the trees. Invisible from the shore. We would have to come up with a plan for scavenging the land once we docked the small boat.

"There's someone on the beach," Smee announced, pointing west.

I followed his hand until my eyes met a man waving his arms in our direction. He looked skinny like a pole and his skin had been tanned very dark by the sun.

He must have been stuck here for a very long time, I thought as I looked at his leathery skin. We had just run our dinghy ashore when he took off running right for us. His movement was erratic, weaving back and forth across the sand as his face broke into a grin.

"I think he's friendly but keep your wits about you," I commanded my men, unsure of the stranger's motives. There wasn't supposed to be anyone else on Barrie according to Bell so I didn't know what to think.

"My friends!" the stranger yelled as he got closer. I could now see that his face was covered with a patchy grey beard, so long I couldn't see his mouth beneath. His arms were stretched wide as he collided with Mullins first. They hit the ground hard as I grabbed my sword, ready for another fight.

"Get off me!" Mullins cried, pushing the man's shoulders from beneath. He rolled off the pirate onto the beach. The strange bloke had only a small cloth covering his waist.

I had a strange feeling that he wasn't all there in the head as he stood back up. The fall didn't seem to affect him at all, his smile still wide as he embraced us all. I looked at him once more as he pulled me in for a hug so tight I struggled to breathe.

Makeshift sandals covered his feet, made from tree bark and something green. It was money, I realized, stepping away as the hug finally ceased. Modern money like I had seen Hanzel use in his time. The bills had been wrapped around the top of his foot, connecting to bark underneath.

"I was beginning to think I would never be found," he explained in a puff. "They must have sent you to rescue me! But

I'm afraid I don't want to go back. I've made a home here for myself and quite like it, you see."

We all stood silent, confused as to what he was talking about. This couldn't be the key to defeating Pan; he must have been marooned on the island for some time, the sun clearly having an effect.

I turned to Smee. His mouth was open like he was about to voice his concern. No words made it out as he remained frozen. Hanzel was usually the one to handle new people so we were a little out of our comfort zone, so to speak.

"We're not here to take you back," I assured the strange man. "You're free to stay here as you please." Although that didn't seem like the safest idea for him, I couldn't argue with what he wanted. We had bigger obstacles to face.

"They didn't send you to bring me back?" he asked, confused. He walked in circles across the sand, his chin held in his hands like he was deep in thought.

"No," Smee began quietly. "We don't know who you are, sir. We have come to this island to finish a quest." His face looked apologetic as he informed the pacing man of our intent.

"What is your name?" I asked, deciding to play along. If he had been here for a while, he would know the land well. Maybe he could be of assistance to us.

"I'm known as D.B., but you can just call me Cooper," he explained, shaking my hand so hard my arm felt like rubber. His eyes went straight to my hook as he pulled his away.

I sighed, knowing he was about to ask what had happened to me. It was always one of the first things people enquired about when we met.

"Nice hook!" Cooper commented with a smile instead.

"Thank you," I mumbled, unsure what to say. He was different than anyone I had met before, blissfully unaware of the danger he faced.

Turning toward the rest of my men, he placed his hands at his sides. "You must all be starving! Come with me," he said simply, immediately turning toward the line of trees at the edge of the beach.

"I'm hungry," Starkey quipped, his eyes full of hope at the promise of a hot meal.

Mullins and Smee turned their eyes to me, unsure of what to do. As my stomach growled in protest at the thought, I realized we had not eaten since yesterday. My instincts told me Cooper was a friendly man so I didn't see any harm in following him home for a meal.

"We'll go to his home to gather our strength," I said to my men, making a final decision, "and find out how well he knows Barrie. He might be able to help us find the rock, and if not, at least we'll have the energy to continue."

"But what if it's a trap?" Smee asked. His eyes held a small dose of fear as he looked at Cooper walking away. We were used to things not going our way so I didn't blame him for being skeptical.

"He won't harm us," I promised. "He has on nothing but a cloth and shoes made out of a tree. There were no weapons on him that could be hidden. We'll be safe if we go to his home, I'm confident of that. My instincts have told me there is nothing evil on the island."

"Come along," came Cooper's voice once again as he stood at the edge of the trees. He looked genuine in his want to help us along and I was thankful that we would soon be able to eat.

Nodding in encouragement to my men once more, I turned and followed. Whatever he made would give us a boost as we were slowly beginning to fade. The events of the last few days were catching up, causing our bodies to droop with fatigue.

As we made our way toward whatever Cooper called home, I noticed the crew beginning to relax.

"So, how did you get here?" Smee asked first, for he was always the curious one.

"I crash landed a few years back," the kooky man explained. "Been stuck here ever since. There were a lot of people looking for me in the beginning I assume, but they never did find me."

"I'm sorry," Starkey said as he patted Cooper on the shoulder. "Was it your family?"

"Ha!" came his sharp laugh in reply. "I don't have any family left, I'm afraid. I was on the run from the police when I disappeared. Jumped right out of a plane with a parachute on my back and ended up here."

I didn't know whether to believe him or not, the story seeming less than likely as he continued.

"I had nothing on me but $200,000 in cash at the time. I'm sure the FBI searched far and wide for my body but they have never been anywhere near here," he bragged. We were now walking up a steep incline, holding the base of each tree as we pulled ourselves up toward the top.

I thought back to his sandals I saw on the beach. I had recognized it being money of some kind, my suspicions of him being from Hanzel's time proving correct. "Where are you from?" I asked, intrigued.

"I'm from the great state of Oregon!" he boasted as he reached the top of the hill. "I was born there in 1939. Grew up there my whole life until I disappeared after hijacking a flight in the 70s."

I had decided he was probably not telling the truth; the story seemed too outlandish to believe. He must have come from some sort of boat, a few dollars on him in his pack. He was friendly enough and seemed to want to make friends so the tale he told wasn't anything more than an anecdote meant to impress us.

"What a story," Smee commented politely. By the look on his face, it was clear he didn't believe Cooper either, but there was no harm in letting him continue.

"It was a messy life," he said with a laugh, turning back toward us as we all reached the top of the hill behind him. "But without it, I wouldn't have found this home, so for that I'm very thankful."

I looked ahead as the land became flat, the trees growing tall above us. I had to shake my head and wipe my eyes, convinced I was seeing a mirage.

There was a small hut just a few paces away, the outside wrapped in nothing but money. The unfamiliar bills were all plastered to the side, from the ground all the way up to the roof. He had even built a little wraparound deck that had the same coating as the rest of the wood.

"It's real," I whispered out loud to myself. The man had been telling the truth.

"Of course, it's real," Cooper said, putting his arm around my shoulder. "Did you not think that I had a home? I think you might have gotten too much sun. Please, take a seat and have some water."

He ushered me to a small stump so that I could sit down, my mind still trying to catch up.

"He has a house made of money?" Starkey said with a grin. "I didn't expect that."

We were all seated on various stumps as Cooper made his way back from within his home. In his hand was a coconut he had cut in half, spilling over with what looked to be water.

"Here you go," he offered, placing the coconut in my good hand. "It's probably a sun stroke so you'll want to drink all of that. You could be dehydrated."

His face was full of concern as I quickly slurped the liquid down my throat.

So, he had been telling the truth after all, I thought. It turned out he wasn't crazy at all.

"Feeling better?" he asked as I finished the drink, placing it on the ground by my feet.

"I am, thank you," I said politely. "I must admit I didn't think you were telling the truth about the adventures you had described. But seeing this home, it's now clear to me that you are exactly who you said."

Cooper laughed, slapping his bare knee at my revelation. "I suppose it does seem a little crazy, doesn't it?" he agreed. "But I assure you, I'm what I told."

I looked at Smee as he coughed, clearing the air so that he could talk.

"We have a favor to ask you," he began. "Just a question, really, but we're hoping you'll be able to help."

It seemed as though my second-in-command had managed to stay on course with the plan. I nodded in approval, thankful that at least one of us was keeping it together.

"Go ahead," Cooper said as he rose once again. "You can ask me while I start dinner."

He grabbed a few vegetables he had stacked to the side of the hut and began chopping them with a rock-knife.

"There's something we're searching for on this island," I began as I watched him grab a large pot. He poured water inside and set it over a fire.

"A rock formation that's shaped like a skull. Have you seen it before?" I asked hopefully. If he had, we would save a lot of time on this quest.

"A skull," Cooper repeated as he thought. He stirred the vegetables into the pot as it bubbled over and steamed. "I think I remember something like that. It's somewhere in that direction," he said, pointing behind the hut. "About an hour's walk from here, I believe. It shouldn't take you that long to find."

My heart exploded with joy as my idea proven to be fruitful. We now knew where to go once we finished eating. The secret of Barrie would soon be ours!

Mullins and Starkey stood up, offering a helping hand as Cooper began scooping the hot food into bowls.

"We're so close, I can taste it." Smee smirked my way. "We have to leave as soon as we're done!"

I couldn't help but grin back as we were handed our hot meal. I quickly thanked Cooper as I began to eat, the crisp vegetables settling my stomach. I didn't realize how hungry I was until my spoon scraped the bottom of the bowl.

"Thank you very much, Cooper," I said to our host. "We would surely be lost without your guidance and food!"

Barking a laugh, he shook his head. "It was my pleasure, gentlemen! While I have loved being alone on this island so far, I do have to admit it was nice to meet you all!"

As we said our goodbyes and gathered our things, I looked at my men once again. The three of them had renewed energy, no doubt because of the food. I still couldn't believe we had come this far, the journey almost coming to an end.

"Take care, my new friends," Cooper said as we prepared to leave. "Maybe someday we'll meet again!"

I smiled and waved as we disappeared through the trees, our eager bodies carrying us forward.

We had made it a few paces ahead when Smee broke the silence. "It seems to be getting very thick just ahead," he commented. "We should pull the walnuts out from your pack."

It was a trick Hanzel had taught us during one of our past adventures when we had found ourselves deep in the forest. He would crack open walnuts with his boots as we walked ahead, leaving a trail to make sure we didn't get lost. I tried to do the same once, but my boots weren't strong enough.

I'll make new boots out of that crocodile, I promised myself.

"Good idea," I acknowledged, handing them to Starkey as he was always the one furthest back. Mullins and Starkey brought up the rear.

Starkey took the bag with a smile, immediately smashing the first nut in his fist.

We all whistled as our swords created a path big enough to walk through. Our spirits were higher than ever before as we made our way toward the rock. I was hoping to reach it before nightfall just in case it was difficult to see.

"We should be there any minute," Smee commented. "The bushes clear just ahead!"

He was standing in front, his sword moving at lightning speed as he chopped all the plants down. I could feel the determination coming off him in waves, causing me to jump ahead with just as much enthusiasm.

"Do you think we'll be able to see it immediately?" Smee asked.

"I hope so," I said passionately. "I'm ready to find out what it is."

I was referring to the secret, of course. I was dying to know what could be powerful enough to finally give us the upper hand. We had people to rescue and a world that needed to be saved.

"As am I!" Smee proclaimed while we watched the final branch take its place at our feet.

I peeked at our new surroundings. There was a beautiful waterfall to my right, sharp rocks poking up in different angles at its base. The water was the same crystal green we had noticed coming ashore, sparkling in the sunset as it tumbled over the edge. It was beautiful.

Behind the waterfall was a wall made of the same rock that stuck out in front. Smee wandered wander around its edge, momentarily distracted by the beauty.

"There are shapes in the wall," he noticed, turning back to me.

I squinted and walked closer to where he stood. When I got closer, I noticed the shape of a ship had formed in the face of the rock. I reached out and touched it, tracing the outline of the smooth vessel.

"There's another one down here," came Mullins' voice. He was standing right behind the fall on a small walkway that had been hiding behind.

Smee and I made our way over to see what other outlines had been formed. My chest inflated like a balloon as I noticed a skull just in front of me.

"This is it," I whispered in awe. Everything had come down to this moment. Whatever was hidden inside this formation would change our lives forever.

Every detail of the skull had been carved by magic into the rock wall. It was incredibly accurate. The eyes and mouth dipped into the stone while the nose had a small opening like a cave. It was small enough that our hands wouldn't fit, leaving me wondering what we were supposed to do.

"The cake," I remembered aloud, pulling my pack from my shoulders. I dug around each pocket, forgetting where I had put Bell's gift.

My hands finally found the clear bag of cakes as my men gathered around me.

"We must eat the cakes and climb inside its nose," I said, pulling four cakes from the bag. I then handed one to each of my men, shoving the last straight into my mouth.

I watched as each of us shrunk, turning into the size of a fist. We climbed the rock up to the nose of the skull, thankful we had just gotten to eat. Our strength pulled us up fast, taking only a few minutes to make it to the hole in the nose.

"Why did the booger cross the deck?" Smee giggled, unable to control himself.

Sighing, I turned to him with a smile. "I have no idea," I said.

"Because he was being picked on." He smiled cheekily. He knew it was a terrible joke but then again, we had never climbed through a nose before.

"You're insufferable sometimes, you know that, Smee?" I laughed.

"I thought it was funny," Starkey objected with a wide grin on his face.

I rolled my eyes as we entered the mouth of the cave, our boots making a sound like we were walking on gravel.

"There's a light at the end," I noticed.

As we got closer, I realized the light was coming from lanterns that hung on the ceiling of the cave, like lights. There was a small kitchen equipped with a stove and a sink against the left side, a bed pressed to the far right. A round table with five chairs sat in the center and a pile of rags laid pushed in the corner.

"It's like a little home," Smee whispered.

"Someone lives here," I agreed.

Humming filled the air as the pile of rags shifted. I immediately realized it wasn't a pile of rags, but a girl picking mushrooms from the floor. When she had gathered all the fungi, she stood up and danced about the room.

"It's as if she's under a spell," Mullins quietly observed. "Does she not notice we're here?"

"I don't know," I replied, wondering the same thing.

She made her way to the stove, slicing the mushrooms into pieces before placing them into a pan. As she continued to hum, she danced to the sink and filled a small cup to the rim. We watched as she poured the water into the pan and stirred the mushrooms as they cooked over the flame.

"Excuse me," I interrupted, hoping to pull her from the spell.

The young woman turned around fast, a surprised look covering her face. "Pardon my manners," she said in an accent. "Would you men like a cup of tea?"

I could now see her clearly as she faced me. Her hair was strung up in a pale blue bow, her matching blue eyes sparkling in the light.

"That would be lovely," Smee said as we all sat down at the table unsure.

She turned to her cupboards, pulling out teacups and saucers, preparing us all tea like we weren't complete strangers.

"Did she know we were coming, or is she in some sort of daze?" Smee whispered, confused. This was not what we were expecting when we had entered the cave.

I didn't reply as I studied our new host.

Her humming grew quieter as she boiled something on the stove, the teapot screeching as an alarm. She grabbed it by the handle and pranced over to where we sat.

As she poured the strange looking tea into our cups, she opened her mouth once again. "I don't have any biscuits I'm afraid, but I'm cooking mushrooms if you would like to wait." She smiled at the floor.

"That's okay," I assured her, gesturing for her to take a seat as we all picked up our cups of tea. I took a small sip, quickly spitting it back out as I realized she had just given us mud.

She boiled mud in her teapot? I asked myself, confused. *She had to be under some sort of spell.*

I looked across the table to Smee, who was giving me a look of bewilderment. "What's going on?" he mouthed.

I shrugged as she finally raised her head, smiling dreamily at all of us.

"How is the tea?" she asked in a stupor, her mind seeming not really there.

214

I busied myself at looking around the walls for maybe a weapon or clue that would help me defeat Pan and his army. It had to be somewhere in this cave. This was the skull Tiger Lily and Bell had mentioned.

"Wonderful," I murmured distractedly. I couldn't see a thing on the wall, nor anywhere in the space surrounding us.

Smee nudged me under the table, pointing to his pocket as a signal. He wanted me to see how much time had passed since we had entered the skull.

I pulled Pan's watch from my pocket, checking the time. As I brought it above the edge of the table to show Smee, the strange girl suddenly squeaked.

Shocked by the sound, I turned to her to see what had alarmed her. She froze at the sight of the watch.

"Do you know this watch?" I asked hopefully.

She slowly reached her hand out toward the watch, the look still catching her eye. I gripped the watch tighter as she moved forward, her eyes snapping up to mine in a hurry.

She looked at me questioningly. "Is that you, Peter?" she asked in a whisper. Her eyes opened wide as I processed her words.

"I'm not Peter," I explained.

"I didn't think so," she said confidently. "You have kind eyes and Peter doesn't."

My heart picked up speed as those words left her mouth. "Who are you?" I asked wishfully.

She smiled, her eyes becoming clear as she stood tall and looked at each of my men before turning back to me.

"I'm Wendy," she introduced herself. "And I'm the one who can help you kill Pan."

TO BE CONTINUED...

EPILOGUE

A Sneak Peek at Book Two

I was standing in my old room eleven years ago, the night before I flew away with Pan. I had learned to control Tiger Lily's clock very well by now, using it to travel almost every night while the rest of my men slept.

Honestly, I didn't know what I was doing here. I just felt like coming to my original home. After everything that had happened recently, I needed to clear my head, and this was the last place I had been as a real child.

I sat in the corner, watching myself sleep. I looked like such a fool back then. I laughed to myself as my snores filled the air and a drop of drool drifted onto the pillow.

The wall shifted, causing me to jump into the closet to hide. I didn't know if someone was coming, like Pan. I didn't know if the watch would react to his past self.

He might have come into my room the night before taking me but I didn't remember waking up.

I watched through the slats of the closet. I noticed something falling from the wall near my bed. It piled up on the floor at a rapid pace.

Why was sand falling from the wall? I wondered to myself incredulously. It didn't make any sense.

As the pile grew larger, it grew legs and soon arms and a body followed. My eyes popped wide open as I realized the sand was forming itself into the shape of a man. He tiptoed to my side, placing his hands on my head, as he closed his eyes dreamily.

Suddenly, I was slammed with a memory, a dream I had that same night.

I was sitting on a bench on the side of the street as I waited for Father to pick me up. He walked this way on his way home and I wanted to surprise him with some pence I had found.

I kicked my legs as a man walked up to me, taking a seat to my left. He had a piece of candy in his hand as he turned to me with an encouraging smile. Nodding at his hand, he gestured for me to take it.

"Thank you, sir," I said excitedly. I was only allowed candy on the most special of occasions so this was a real treat.

"My name is Sandman," he introduced himself. "Are you enjoying your dream?"

"My dream?" I asked the strange man. "I'm not dreaming. I'm awake. I'm waiting for my Father, you see."

"Ah, but you are dreaming, dear boy, for I am the Sandman. And it's my job to power all the children's dreams," he informed me. *He held out his hand for me to take as we began walking down the street, the road suddenly becoming bright green grass.*

"See, I have just changed your dream," he said. We were now sitting in a meadow, the wind cooling my skin blissfully. "For you can see anything that you want to see, you just have to let yourself believe."

I can control my own dreams? *I thought as I imagined a tiny blue bird. As I opened my eyes, a small bird with blue feathers chirped my name on a branch just above.*

It spoke to my delight "Hello, James. Can I be your friend?"

"Yes!" I yelled immediately. I had always wanted a pet bird, but my father had told me no every time.

The Sandman stood up, petting the bird on the head and donning a hat that he didn't have before.

"I just wanted to stop in and make sure that your dreams are as happy as can be," he said with another smile. "Because they should always be what you want them to be. Remember that, James."

And with that, he was gone.

I shook my head at the memory, enraged at the thought of Sandman coming to save me. For a second, I had believed I would never have a bad dream, but I was very wrong.

I grabbed the clock, planning to head straight to the window as soon as he disappeared into the wall. But as his hands pulled away from my head, I noticed another disturbance in the mirror above my long dresser.

In the blink of an eye, Pan shot through the sphere and landed silently on the floor of my bedroom. The Sandman didn't notice as Pan snuck up behind him with a bucket of water in both hands.

Without thinking, I made a noise in the closet, trying to warn Sandman of the danger. He quickly turned around, surprising Pan who jumped backward as he realized he had been caught.

"Put the water down, Pan," Sandman warned.

Regaining his composure, my nemesis stepped closer to the edge of the bed. "Give me what I came here for and we won't have a problem." He smiled. "I've been following you around for a very long time and won't go home empty-handed."

Sandman raised his arms in a motion of forfeit as he grabbed a sack from his belt. "Take it. I know it's the sand that you want. You will use it to control other boys' dreams," he spat.

"Oh, I'll take much more than that." Pan laughed darkly. He snapped his fingers in the dark room, setting the bucket on the floor. "I was just going to kill you and steal the bag," he began as a few of his fairy guards flew from the mirror. "But now I have a different idea."

"Please, just take the sand," Sandman begged. "I haven't done anything to you. I don't know why you've been hunting me down."

Ignoring his pleas, Pan grabbed his sword from his sash and spoke to the fairies with ease. "Get your bags ready," he commanded. "This is going to make quite the mess."

The Sandman dropped to his knees as Pan pierced him in the heart, his body turning to dust instantly. As it fell on the floor, the fairies flew in close and scooped the dust into their bags.

I watched with my hand over my mouth as I realized Pan had come to see me earlier than I believed. My young body tossed and turned from a nightmare as he came close to my face and took a deep breath.

"Mmmm...," he murmured almost inaudibly. His grin spread from side to side as he opened his mouth in ecstasy.

"I can taste his weakness from here," he said aloud to the fairies. "He is perfect."

My body grew cold as I shivered in fear. The evil in Pan continued to astound me each time I saw him, but this was by far the most disturbing.

As a child, I had no idea that such evil had found me while I labored in sleep. I continued to toss and turn as my nightmare carried me away.

"Are you having a bad dream, dear one?" He smirked icily. He grabbed the bag of sand and sprinkled his hands, placing them on my forehead.

I was immediately sucked in by another memory of that same dream.

Sandman had disappeared with a tip of his hat, and I began carrying a conversation with the bird.

"What is your name?" I asked. "Can I call you Big Blue?"

The bird laughed, its beak clicking in song as it nodded at my enthusiasm. "You can call me whatever you want, my dear boy. I'm yours to keep, therefore, I'm yours to name!"

I stood up and grabbed the bird, placing its tiny feet on my arm. "Hold on tight!" I told the bird, an idea forming in my head.

I bent my knees and jumped as high as I could, imagining what it would be like to fly. I had always wondered how fast it would be, and as I steered through the sky, I felt happier than I ever could have imagined.

It was amazing! I could see the town bustling below, the wind whipping through my short hair. I weaved my body back and forth as I dipped through the trees, feeling elated as I realized the Sandman was right.

"I can do anything I want!" I yelled to Big Blue and the sky. The bird hopped from my arm and took off in flight, keeping pace with me as we raced to the sun.

"What do you want to do next?" it asked, its face full of joy. It seemed like it was having just as much fun.

I thought to myself for a minute, wondering what could be better than flying.

"Let's go find Father!" I announced to the bird. I closed my eyes, imagining him on his boat. He was always in the best mood when he was onboard.

I opened my eyes once again as I spotted the vessel, sailing on the calm waters below.

"Father, I can fly! Look up here, in the sky!" I yelled as we made our way close.

He turned my way with a big smile on his face, waving and cheering me on. Trying to impress him, I flew faster than before, an idea brewing in my head to try a flip mid-air. His cheering grew louder as I turned upside down and completed the circle in one try.

"That was great, James. I'm so proud!" he cheered, steering the wheel out to sea.

Filled with glee, I turned toward the open water, noticing a group of grey clouds headed straight for the ship.

"Be careful, Father. I see a storm headed this way. You should turn back for the day and come home with me," I suggested.

But he didn't listen to me. He just continued ahead as if I had said nothing at all. "Father," I repeated again, confused as to what was going on.

"It's time to wake up," Big Blue warned, slowing down. "This dream is not safe anymore."

Fear bloomed in my chest as I turned to the bird. "What do you mean? Sandman said I could control my dreams. Nobody else had the power but me."

"There is something stronger at play," it protested. "Please, open your eyes. It's time to wake up."

I looked at Big Blue's eyes as they pleaded with me, choosing to ignore them instead. Nothing that bad could come from a dream. I had my father with me, at least.

"It's okay, little one," I argued with the bird. "I'm safe, I promise. We can keep flying around until morning wakes me back up."

Without another word, I flew straight for Father's boat. "Father, let us go home. I'm hungry and want something to eat."

I imagined a big plate of ham.

"Quiet, you stupid boy!" his voice rang out, causing my eyes to pop open in fear. His face was bright red with anger as he stepped closer to me. "You think I work all day and I slave all night just so that you can eat all my food?" he screamed, spit flying everywhere.

"I... I don't know what you're talking about," I stammered. I didn't mean it like that. He had to know that.

"You are selfish and vile! I have always hated your presence," he admitted. "I wish you had never been born!"

I began to cry at his words as they punctured my soul, my throat ripping wide open in sobs.

This wasn't like him, even in real life. He would never get this mad at me. I drew my eyebrows down low, confused, as I tried to figure out how to regain control of my dream.

I looked up once more, deciding that apologizing would be the best way to go. But as I opened my mouth, everything around me froze in time.

Maybe this is what happens when a dream switches off, *I said to myself hopefully. I wanted to wake up because I was no longer having fun.*

"Turn around," *came a dreadful voice from behind, causing chills to creep up my arms. I slowly turned toward the sound. Whoever it was, they didn't seem friendly.*

To my surprise, there stood a boy a few years older than me. His clothes were all green and his spiky hair looked almost orange as it caught the rays of the sun.

"Your father is very vicious," *he observed nosily.* "He has done this a lot, has he not?"

Bawling my hands into fists, my veins filled with fire as his words sent me into a rage. "He has not," *I argued back.* "He has never said such words to me! You don't know us, why are you here?"

His face turned red as I screamed the words in his face, his rage quickly catching up to mine.

"I encourage you not to talk to me like that again," *he said quietly as a deadly look crossed his face and his head tipped to the side like a cat.*

But I didn't listen. I let the anger explode out of me instead.

"Leave! Me! Alone!" I shouted each word between breaths as I poked his chest.

"You will regret this one day. I promise you that. I will give you one more chance to behave," he said calmly. He took one step back and crossed his arms, waiting for me to make the next move.

"I love my father," I explained, starting to calm down. "I don't know why you even care. It's not like I have anything to do with you."

"Oh, but that's where you are wrong." The strange boy laughed, slowly walking over to my father.

"Someday you will do everything I ask," he explained. "You have no choice because I have the power."

Confused by his words, I let the seconds tick by as I tried to organize my thoughts.

"But this is just a dream, so you can't control me," I concluded. "When I wake up, everything will be okay."

The boy circled the deck, jumping onto the wheel. He looked giddy with joy as if he already had the upper hand.

"That's no longer true," he said, eyes turning black. "I have the power to control all of you."

"What do you mean, you have the power to control me?" I asked in disbelief. "I've never even met you." His words

228

weren't making sense to me, throwing me off. I just wanted to wake up so that I could shake it off.

His hand moved suddenly as I jumped to the ground in fear. I didn't know what he tried to throw at me, only that it had hit my face in an explosion of muck.

"Did you throw dirt at me?" I asked as I coughed, the dust causing me to choke on the air.

"You will obey me," he repeated. "You will do what I say, do you understand?"

I felt funny as my body began to tingle, my head feeling fuzzy and numb. "I will obey you," I said dumbly, no control over my brain. "You have the power and I don't."

"That's better," he said as he walked close to me again. "Now, listen and do what I command."

I nodded my head and leaned in with my ear, waiting for his word to show me the way.

"You will forget that you met me, you will forget this part of the dream. Do you understand?" he asked sharply.

"I understand," I replied automatically.

"You will remember that you hate your father, and want to run away," he continued. "He has hurt you before and he will do it again," he lied. "Your life is nothing but sadness and sorrow."

I repeated his words in the simplest of tones, still left without control of my thoughts.

"I will come to your room tomorrow when you have fallen asleep, and I will offer a chance at a better life. You will take it because you hate home so much," he said smugly, gloating.

"I will go wherever you want to take me," I spoke softly. "For you know what is best for my life and everyone."

He laughed uncontrollably, the only sound filling the air as our surroundings were still frozen in time. Although I couldn't control my mind or body, somewhere inside of me deep I could feel the coldness sinking in like stone.

"When I clap my hands, you will do everything I have said," he said as he circled me. "And I will be gone from your brain all at once."

I stood silently as he stopped in front of me, bringing his hands together with as much force as he could muster.

Smack*! The loud noise cracked the air as the world around me turned black.*

I took a deep breath as the dream faded away, the memory suddenly returning all at once. What had caused me to finally remember, I had no idea, but I now knew the first night with Pan had been a lie.

My father wasn't the monster I had thought him to be because Pan had manipulated my thoughts. I could only assume it was fairy dust that he used to put me under a spell, but whatever it was had not been powerful enough to stop me from remembering tonight in the closet.

I watched as Pan pulled his hand from my sleeping body, his laughter echoing once again. "That was too easy," he bragged to the fairies as they cleaned. "I will use him until his blood runs dry."

He continued laughing as he gathered his things and followed the fairies back through the mirror to Neverland. There wasn't a doubt in my mind that he had used the same dust on Smee.

He probably traveled into his dreams and messed up his mind, making him forget all about his family, I thought to myself.

I started to sweat as I thought of breaking the news to Smee, not even knowing where to begin. Pan was capable of doing more evil things than we had thought possible.

It had taken me almost eleven years to realize he had been playing games with me since he laid eyes upon my face. I had fallen for his tricks much harder than I thought. Once again, he had broken the scale.

I needed to get back to Smee and the others to warn them of this new information. I didn't know how this would change the plan, but it meant we had even more at stake. I thought avenging the death of my family and friends while saving all of Neverland was more than enough, but now there was more to defend.

As I snuck back out of the closet and outside to get some fresh air, I couldn't help but feel numb from everything I had seen. Pan would have no idea I knew because he didn't see me, but he would be livid once he found out.

"We must figure out a way to use it against him somehow," I thought aloud as I climbed a nearby building. I quickly ran to the edge, jumping with all my might toward the ground.

Tiger Lily's clock exploded with light, sucking me in to take me back home.

***

"Wake up!" I screamed, pounding on all the doors of the ship. "Wake up! I have something to share!"

Smee poked his head out, blinking with sleep as he noticed me frantic stare. "What's wrong?" he said groggily.

Wendy stepped from her room next, a strange look on her face. "Something has happened," she said observantly. "Please tell us what is going on."

"I know how Pan has been finding me in my dreams," I announced to them both. "But we have a bigger problem."

"What' s that?" Smee asked, alarm crossing his face. They were listening intently to what I was saying.

"It isn't just mine he is capable of finding," I began carefully. With a deep breath, I looked at each one of their faces, dreading what I had to say next. "He's able to jump into any child's mind he pleases, and he is powerful enough to alter their mind."

ABOUT THE AUTHOR

C. L. Bush started reading at a young age. Since then she has voraciously read all she could get her hands on. She has a degree in Business and is a mother of two boys and three grown stepdaughters, as well as the wife of a soldier in the U.S. Army. Her life is busy, but she has always kept her love of reading and writing alive. History is also a passion of hers, and she regularly goes on trips with her family to experience it firsthand. She looks forward to bringing her love of reading, writing, and history to her readers.

Contact her on Facebook:

www.facebook.com/authorclbush/

Or at her website: www.clbush.com

OTHER BOOKS BY C.L. BUSH

Fire In My Heart Series:

The Heart of Now – Book One

Fire of My Past – Book Two

Wife of Tomorrow – Book Three

A Hand in Love and Murder – Book Four

A Trial of Secrets – Book Five

A Vindicated Heart – Book Six

Major Series:

Major Bodyguard – Book One

Major Pacifier – Book Two

Major Charming – Book Three

Stand Alones:

Alice and Uncas

Echo of Whispers Series:

Echo of Whispers – Book One

*I F*cking Love Coloring Series:*

Mandala 1st Edition

Mandala 2nd Edition

American/UK Cuss Word Edition

Made in the USA
Lexington, KY
10 December 2018